The Byram Su

Mira Stables

For Muriel

Table of Contents

Chapter One

"Now pray don't fall into one of your takings, my love," begged Mrs. Newton apprehensively. "It will not be so *very* bad, I promise you. I will admit that when Papa first broached the scheme I could not help feeling that you would not like it. But I have given a good deal of thought to it since then and I fancy it will do very well."

Miss Albertine Newton's beautiful eyes held an angry sparkle. "Do very well," she mimicked crossly. Her mother flinched, and closed her own eyes. Best let the child vent her temper before resuming the attempt to make her see reason, since she would do so in any case. And how magnificent she looked, even in her anger, thought her doting Mama, stealing a cautious peep beneath lowered lids at the fulminating goddess who was striding up and down her bedroom floor in most unfeminine fashion as she poured out her angry tirade. It was a pity, though, that she permitted passion to mar the soft pretty voice so carefully cultivated by a long succession of governesses. Her mother knew from experience that it would be useless to try persuasion or even bribery until that strident note had abated.

"— how he could devise so outrageous a scheme, or you consent to it," her daughter fumed. "Why should I be burdened with the milky-mouthed chit? So meek and so biddable — such a pattern-card of maidenly behaviour! I have always disliked her. And since Cousin Albert left her all his money I have positively detested her. *I* was the one who was saddled with his perfectly horrible name. The least he could have done by way of making amends was to leave me his fortune. Surely it was in hopes of just such a honeyfall that you named me as you did? I can think of no other reason! Albertine! Pah! It would take every penny of eighty thousand pounds to sweeten such a nauseous dose. And then he leaves it all to dear little Cousin Alethea, because, forsooth, her 'modest demeanour and steadfast principles have earned his respect and affection', whereas I — I, his godchild and namesake — 'appear to stand in no need of wealth, being already so richly endowed with beauty, brains and spirit'. The old

7

curmudgeon! Just because I set him to rights once or twice about his management of his servants, who were utterly spoiled and idle."

Mrs. Newton shuddered, remembering that last disastrous visit — the one which had caused dear Cousin Albert to change his Will. She herself had been sincerely attached to him, but naturally Albertine — and she must remember to call her Tina — had been out of humour at being dragged away from Town at the very height of her first season to wait upon the whims of a sick man. Cousin Albert had taken a fancy to have Maria and her daughter visit him for a while and nothing else would serve. Maria had protested their many engagements but the invalid, being convalescent, was inclined to be cantankerous. Parties and pleasurings could wait a little while. His godchild had all the best years of her life ahead of her while he was tottering on the brink of the grave. Surely they could spare a sennight, if no more, to cheer and hearten a frail old man who had but little pleasure left in life? And partly from sheer good-heartedness and partly because she had, indeed, nourished hopes that her daughter would inherit a part at least of that very handsome fortune, Maria had yielded to his wish.

She had regretted it bitterly. Albertine — the dear child was so young, so ingenuous, with not a thought for her own advantage or the punishment that her wilful behaviour might incur — had run the whole gamut of temperamental display from sullen rudeness to frank insolence. It was some time, now, since Maria had done more than try to manoeuvre her beautiful daughter into her more charming moods, and in this case her best efforts had proved unavailing. It was questionable which of the three of them was the most thankful when the visit ended.

"— the only sensible thing he did was to die at the right time," said the sharp voice, and Mrs. Newton noticed automatically that the fury was subsiding. "But if you and Papa imagine that I shall permit my *second* season to be ruined because he would like me to nursemaid my cousin, you are sadly mistaken. You at least, Mama, are not without understanding. I have my own circle of friends and I will not impose upon them by attempting to foist my dull and dowdy cousin into their ranks."

Mrs. Newton hastened to seize upon this promising opening. "No, indeed, my love. That would be *very* bad," she said eagerly, "and quite unnecessary. Your cousin is used to quiet country living and could never endure the hectic round of gaiety that *your* season is likely to offer," she went on with fond pride. "Papa wishes me to give an evening party to present her to the 'ton' and you will enjoy *that*, you know. I have been thinking about it, and it struck me that your cousin's quiet ways and unobtrusive appearance would be an excellent foil for my darling's gay vivacity."

The last embers of wrath were extinguished. "Not that I need a foil to set me off, but there is something in what you say," allowed her darling critically. "Though I don't see why her parents cannot hire a house in Town for the season and take charge of her début themselves. Why should *you* be put to all the pains of chaperoning another fledgeling?"

Much encouraged by this unlooked for solicitude, Mrs. Newton explained that Uncle Clement could not abandon the care of his parish and that Aunt Verona's delicate health made it impossible for her to undertake a prolonged sojourn in Town without his support. "Since her last illness, you know, the least exertion beyond the common quite knocks her up. If she had been in full health Alethea would have been brought out last year, but it was judged wiser to wait until Susan was of an age to supply the care and companionship that her Mama will miss when Alethea comes to us."

"Also, last year, she had not inherited a fortune, and plain and dull as she is could scarcely hope to make an advantageous marriage. Now I suppose she will flourish her money-bags and shine us all down."

"No, no, my dear," soothed Mama. "Nothing of *that* kind. No one is to know of her inheritance. Her parents would not for worlds expose her to the lures of fortune hunters. While as for making an advantageous marriage, Verona herself assured me that they had no such thought in mind. It is just that they wish her to learn how to conduct herself in society. And despite her birth you must see that she has little enough chance of that at home, what with a mother too frail to take her about and a father too close to being a saint to care for worldly things. I shall take her to a few quiet parties where she will feel more at home than at the more dashing affairs that *you* prefer. Almack's perhaps, if I can obtain vouchers. And I daresay she will enjoy going to the theatre. Clement has no objection to *that*, although he did say he trusted that the chosen piece would be of a moral or instructive nature and I'm sure I don't know" — She broke off, a puzzled frown creasing her pretty, placid brow as she mentally reviewed the current theatrical attractions, none of which exactly fulfilled her brother-in-law's stipulations. "Perhaps Shakespeare," she said doubtfully, and turned again to the far more urgent business of pacifying her daughter.

"Verona has asked me to choose an entire new wardrobe for the child," she began tentatively, "and not to skimp on anything. She knows how demanding a season can be." A petulant pout welcomed this opening gambit. She went on hurriedly, "It will mean the most *lavish* orders for Madame Denise — and then there will be hats, from Serena. I shall drop a hint — in the most delicate way, of course — that they cannot expect such generous patronage without making some return. Such arrangements are perfectly commonplace. I daresay they will make substantial reductions in the cost of your gowns and bonnets. And since Papa has tightened his purse strings and vows you are too spendthrift by half, that will be a great relief to me. For I really could not endure to have you go shabby, my love."

Anything less shabby than the appearance presented by Miss Newton would have been difficult to imagine. From shining red-gold curls to the tips of her little kid slippers she might have posed for an illustration in the Mirror of Fashion. Yet Mrs Newton had good reason for her earnest declamation. Though it was an abiding grief to her that Providence had seen fit to bless her with but the one pledge of her husband's affection, yet she took comfort in the knowledge that her only daughter was quite the loveliest girl in Town. Perhaps, if one preferred dark beauties, Lady Rosalie Hawtrey might be accounted her equal. Certainly she had no superior. Melting hazel eyes beneath slender dark brows, a wild rose complexion rarely seen in a redhead and a delectable figure, added up to a degree of feminine witchery that was potent indeed. Prolonged study might have revealed that, in repose, the rosy lips were too thin for perfect beauty; that the rounded white chin held promise of developing in maturity into lines of aggression strongly reminiscent of its owner's formidable sire. But since the lips were usually composed into pretty pout or seductive smile and the chin sported a wayward dimple, there were few to note these minor defects. Any mother must feel that such perfection should go fittingly clad.

Regrettably, Papa held other views. His fortune was substantial. His household was furnished with comfort and elegance, his table supplied with the finest wines and every seasonable delicacy in addition to plain honest fare and he maintained a smart landaulet for the use of the ladies of the household as well as the town carriage. His wife and daughter were given what he considered adequate pin money. But he examined the household accounts with scrupulous care each month and any unwarrantable increase was sharply questioned. He was proud of his pretty daughter but he had equipped her at considerable expense for her début and it seemed to him unreasonable that he should be expected to disburse further large sums. All those slippers and fans and gloves could not possibly be worn out, to say nothing of a cloak lined with ermine that was fit for a princess, while a good manager would devise ways of refurbishing gowns so that they could be worn again without incurring the stigma of dowdiness or penny pinching.

At the heart of the matter was his disappointment that Albertine had not crowned her successful first season by accepting one of the several very eligible offers which she had received. He was prepared to come down handsomely in the matter of settlements and would have liked to see the girl comfortably established in a home of her own. He had a vague notion that his own home would be a more comfortable place when that happy dénouement was achieved. His wife might speak of youthful high spirits and childish thoughtlessness, and one naturally left the upbringing of a girl to her mama, but for his part he would rather see a peaceful going-on than the alternating raptures, tantrums and sulks to which his daughter was addicted.

The thought of new gowns obtained without having to wheedle them out of Papa did much to reconcile Miss Newton to her cousin's coming. So long as she was not expected to dance attendance on the visitor she was prepared to tolerate her presence. Indeed there were times when it might be quite advantageous to have Mama's attention diverted from her own activities. It was not as though Alethea was likely to attract interest. She was just a brown mouse of a girl, thought Tina contemptuously, whose presence could be discounted. She began to wear a more complaisant air, and though a slight set-back was caused by Mama's rejection of her idea that some of her less successful dresses should be altered to fit her cousin so that she might have new ones, she quite understood the case when Mama explained that the bills for Alethea's gowns would be sent to Papa, he having been named with Uncle Clement as trustee under Cousin Albert's Will.

She even endured with comparative patience a close inquisition as to her plans for the day, and grew only a little restless when Mama pressed for an account of the proceedings at Almack's on the previous evening. Since Mama had been obliged to journey into Kent to complete the arrangements for Alethea's visit, she had entrusted her daughter to the chaperonage of her close friend and neighbour, Mrs. Grayson, who would in any case be in charge of her own daughter, Marianne. Mrs. Grayson was eminently trustworthy and Mama could perfectly rely upon Tina's behaving very prettily. Her only anxiety was that some undesirable gentleman might attempt to scrape acquaintance with her while Mama was not there to ward off such dangerous marauders. There were plenty of them, even at so select a gathering as that presided over by Mr. Willis. By virtue of their birth they might be socially acceptable, but impecunious junior officers and handsome scapegrace younger sons were not suitable friends for her precious Tina.

Had she been less besotted she might have spared her pains. Tina set a far higher value on her charms than even her Mama had ever dreamed of. With prudent forethought that should have pleased her Papa she had carefully evaluated the matrimonial value of all the eligible bachelors. A dazzling smile, the hint of a wistful sigh, she might bestow, but that was all they would have of her, those charming but impecunious young men. Mama's anxious exhortations were quite superfluous.

With obvious patience she rehearsed the names of her partners, those with whom she had exchanged polite small talk and those who had merely bowed to her. In rather more detail she described the gowns she had seen and the compliments that had been paid to her upon her own appearance.

Mama was satisfied up to a point. "Was not Sir John Boothroyd present?" she enquired wistfully. Sir John had been her favourite of Tina's suitors, a pleasant-mannered young man, moderately good looking and not overburdened with brains but possessed of a comfortable fortune and heir to a beautiful old manor where she could just picture her lovely daughter queening it as châtelaine.

"He was there, Mama, but he did not ask me to dance."

"Did he dance more than once with any other lady?" asked Mrs. Newton.

"He did not dance at all," reported Tina, a smile of demure triumph curving her mouth. "Indeed I cannot imagine why he troubled to attend, since whenever I chanced to glance in his direction he was just standing watching m — the company," she substituted hastily.

Mrs. Newton hesitated, studying the lovely face carefully. Tina was half smiling, content, a cream-fed cat look. She risked it. "Could you not bring yourself to reconsider his offer?" she ventured. "I pity him sincerely, such devotion as he has shown."

"And so dull as he is," retorted her daughter swiftly. "No, Mama, I could not. I never encouraged him — you *know* I would not do anything so bold and fast. And a mere baronet will not do for me, especially one who would bore me to distraction before the honeymoon was out. I was born for a higher destiny."

For once Mrs. Newton was shocked. "My child! My angel! What *can* you mean?" she implored.

"Why — nothing in particular, Mama." The angel-child smiled brilliantly. "At least — no particular person. But I cannot help knowing that I am beautiful. Also, though I am at some pains to hide the fact, that I am not without intelligence. Do you not agree that I was born to grace a nobler establishment than Sir John's?"

And leaving her stunned parent to assimilate this disclosure of her ambitions she curtsied gracefully and withdrew in good order.

Chapter Two

Damon leaned back in the corner of the coach, one long leg outstretched to rest comfortably on the opposite seat, one elbow propped against the window so that the hand might shield his scarred cheek. Presently he would become aware that he had fallen once more into this over-dramatic, self-pitying attitude and the hand would be resolutely removed.

Meanwhile he was contemplating his immediate future with bitter distaste. Tonight would not be so bad. A quiet dinner with Kit in his rooms and then a box at the theatre. A box, where one could always withdraw into the shadows if the stares of the curious became too intrusive. But after that — well — he had given his promise and he would keep it, though the prospect appalled him. It was not as though he would be able to live quietly. If he was to achieve his purpose he must enter into all the distractions offered by the season, must see and be seen, ride, dance, converse. And he knew his world well enough to realise that there would be many eyes, hopeful — speculative, upon his every movement. All the match-making mamas would know that the Duke of Byram's heir was looking about him for a wife. Such a situation could never be comfortable. In his peculiar circumstances it was little less than purgatory.

He shifted his position irritably and wondered why Judd should be permitting the horses to take this easy stretch at a walk. At this rate he was going to be late for his dinner engagement. But before he could make enquiry the coach stopped altogether and a moment or two later Judd's melancholy countenance presented itself at the window.

"Road's blocked, milord," he announced gloomily. "There's Parman's Tunbridge Wells stage all across it and a curricle with a smashed wheel on its side in the ditch."

"If there's a stage coach involved there'll be more than enough eager helpers to clear up the mess without our putting ourselves about," said Damon indifferently. "Get on as soon as you can. You'll have to spring 'em a bit when chance offers to make up time."

Judd touched his hat in acknowledgement and retired to his box. If he was a trifle disappointed that his lordship had not required him to go forward and see what aid he could render, thus permitting him a closer view of the smash, he accepted it philosophically. He had expected nothing else. In the space of six months he had learned that Lord Skirlaugh avoided all unnecessary contact with his fellows. It was a pity, thought Judd, who, behind his slightly simian and mournful countenance, was actually a gregarious soul, but one couldn't blame him. There was that silly besom in Watford, for instance, who had screamed blue murder at sight of milord's face, and he, poor soul, not thinking of himself, just springing forward to help her up because she had tripped and fallen and spilled all the parcels out of her basket. Judd would not easily forget the look on his master's face, or the voice in which he had been bidden to help the wench. He would rather have given her a piece of his mind but had not dared to do so lest his lordship should hear him.

He sucked his teeth reflectively and meditated on the ways of foolish women who cared so much for the outside of the cup and platter and little enough for what was within. His young lordship was as decent a lad as ever stepped, careful of his cattle and considerate of his servants. And a pleasant way with him of saying, 'Thank you,' for a man's services, just as though he wasn't well paid to render them. Judd was steadily coming to the opinion that in taking service with him he had made a very good move.

Evidently the accident was not of a serious nature, for it was not much more than twenty minutes before the stage coach came thundering down the road, its driver obviously anxious to make up for lost time acknowledging their presence with a cheerful twirl of his whip. Judd set his horses in motion, but held them to a walk. There was still the smashed curricle to negotiate and the road took a sharp turn to the left. That had probably caused the first accident. There was no telling what might be coming the other way, and *he* had no desire to end up in the ditch.

He edged his way neatly past the wreck and was just about to urge the team to greater speed when a young lady ran out into the road, waving to him to stop, and he perceived that a post-chaise was drawn up at the side of the road just in front of the curricle. A young man was stretched out on the grassy bank that bordered the road, an older female was kneeling beside him, chafing his hands in a rather ineffective way, and a postilion, wearing an air of sullen defiance, was announcing to the ambient air his determination to bide with his horses and not go for no doctor, which likely there wasn't one any way.

15

"Oh! Please will you help me?" begged the lady breathlessly. "Or perhaps your master will be so kind," she added a swift glance having shown that the solitary occupant of the coach was a gentleman. "This poor young man! He vowed he wasn't hurt and indeed he seemed all right save for the bump on his head. One of the stage coach passengers gave him some cordial to drink from a flask that he had providentially placed in his pocket and it seemed to do him good at the time. Then, just after the stage drove off he suddenly collapsed. Miss Hetherstone and I have tried all we know to bring him round but nothing serves and the post boy won't go for a doctor though I begged him to. Do you think your master would permit you to do so? Is he in great haste to push on? Something should be done for this poor man, even though the accident was quite his own fault."

"You could ask him, miss," said Judd doubtfully, and then, as she turned to do so, hitched up the reins and sprang down from the box. It might be less awkward for both parties if *he* did the explaining.

Damon, impatiently aware of further delay and some kind of argument going on in the road, had just leaned forward to lower the window when the two appeared outside it. Seeing a strange female he sank back hastily, averting his head and gazing straight in front of him as Judd gave a brief account of the mishap. To the watching girl he looked insufferably proud and bored. And when, instead of getting out of the coach and going to see what he could do to help, he only directed the coachman to try and discover what ailed the fellow, mounting indignation spilled over into rash words.

"I wouldn't have asked your help, milord" — she had heard Judd address him so — "if I had known you were so puffed up with your own importance," she told him. "How shocking that your journey should be delayed by anything so commonplace as an accident. Pray forgive me! Being myself a person of no importance at all, I wasn't even aware that gentlemen of your consequence did not so much as deign to glance at such inferiors as ventured to approach them."

She regretted the outburst as soon as it was made. Not that he didn't deserve every syllable and a good deal more beside, but it was certainly not her place to take him to task, and ripping up at him in that ill-bred fashion was scarcely the way to engage his assistance for the unfortunate traveller.

For a moment it seemed as though the toplofty gentleman in the coach meant to ignore her remarks as completely as he had ignored her presence. Certainly he did not turn his head or look at her. But after a distinct pause, which left her fidgeting uncomfortably from one foot to the other wondering whether to go off after the coachman or stay where she was to outface her antagonist, he said cuttingly, "Your youth must serve as an excuse for your lack of conduct. One can only trust that you will study to behave more seemly when your schooldays are done. Meanwhile do not let me keep you from one who undoubtedly stands in more need of feminine assistance than I do."

Fortunately, by the time that she had drawn breath adequate to the task of annihilation, Judd came running back. At the sound of the pounding footsteps the gentleman in the coach shed his air of indolence. "Serious?" he snapped, jumping down into the road without bothering to let down the steps.

"Yes, m'lord. At least, no — not the gentleman. *He's* no more than dead drunk — half-sprung to start with, by what the post-boy says, and some fool on the stage knew no better than to pour half a pint of Hollands into him. It's one of his horses. The poor brute is bleeding pretty badly from a gash in his breast. No one thought to look to them save to free them from the wreckage."

The haughty gentleman might have appeared indifferent to the claims of suffering humanity but it was at once apparent that he had a softer heart for the animal kingdom. His long legs carried him swiftly enough to the scene of the accident and after one appraising glance he began issuing a string or orders, bidding Judd make haste and bring him clean linen from his valise — shirts would do — something to make a pad to bind over the wound. The post-boy, peremptorily bidden to go to the poor creature's head, objected sullenly, vowing that the brute was savage. It had already tried to bite him once, and him only doing his best to get it clear of the tangle of harness.

"And a sad pity he didn't succeed," snapped milord. "But he's in no case to bite you now, poor devil. You will be perfectly safe. He's a valuable animal, too. I've no doubt his owner will reward you handsomely for your help in saving him."

"Him!" snorted the post-boy in accents of deep disgust. "Him — as had no more sense than try to pass me on that bend with never a thought for what might be coming the other way? Drunk as a lord, the young care-for-naught. And hard-working lads like me, with a living to earn, we gets blamed if there's a haccident. It's never the quality's fault — oh no! blood

kin to half the magistrates in the county, *they* be. His sort isn't fit to drive an army mule, let alone high-couraged cattle like these."

"On that head I find myself in complete agreement with your sentiments," said milord pleasantly, realising that a good deal of the post-boy's contumacious attitude might be set down to the shock of his own narrow escape and to shame that he had not noticed the animal's injury. "Very well, then, do it to oblige me, there's a good fellow."

To the entire amazement of one, at least, of the bystanders, the post-boy gave a shamefaced grin, and obliged. Judd having returned with his lordship's valise, the two of them set to work to bind a firm pad in place over the ugly looking wound. It proved an awkward task. The horse was young and nervous, and even in his weakened state he resented the handling of strangers, plunging feebly just when he was most required to keep still. Moreover the first makeshift bandage was too short to fasten securely and the job was all to do again.

Obsessed as he was by the need to have his swab in place before the animal lost too much blood, Damon scarcely noticed at what point a fourth assistant joined the party. He snatched thankfully at the length of linen that Judd handed him without pausing to enquire where it came from, and passed it about the horse's body. This time it was amply long enough for his purpose. But it was not until Judd took one end from him to pull it taut that he realised that the hands holding the pad in position were small and white for all their firm efficiency, and that the impudent young hoyden who had taken him to task for his manners was standing quite coolly almost under the animal's forefeet, her cheek pressed to the quivering neck, a crooning murmur of nonsensical endearments issuing from the same soft lips that had been so prompt to pour insults upon *him*. However, this was no time to be considering feminine sensibilities and the wench seemed to know what she was about. Damon dismissed her from his thoughts and concentrated on the adjustment and tightening of the linen that was holding the pad in place.

"He should do now," he said finally, standing back and surveying the patient with a critical eye. "I've seen animals worse wounded recover completely. But he'll need good care for a few days. How about his owner?"

They turned with one accord to survey the curricle driver, a nattily attired young gentleman of some nineteen or twenty summers, who lay in the blissful abandon of drunken slumber, his cheek resting on a stone as confidingly as though it were his pillow. The middle-aged female who had been tending him when the rescue party arrived on the scene had retired to the post chaise and, for some inexplicable reason, had removed several portmanteaux from it. She was now engaged on repacking these, an unusual, not to say inadvisable proceeding on a gusty March day with lowering clouds promising a downpour at any moment. So intrigued was Damon by this eccentric behaviour that he momentarily forgot his disfigurement as he stared at her. By the time it had dawned upon him that that useful roll of linen had come out of one of those portmanteaux both the girl and the post-boy were gazing elsewhere. The muttered oath of the one, the sharply indrawn breath of the other had passed unnoticed.

He stooped over the slumbering youth and shook him roughly but without effect.

"It's no kind of use, guvnor," opined the post-boy. "I reckon he was lushy to start with, else he wouldn't have gone for to pass me just there, and then some cove on the stage gave him gin to pull him together."

Damon nodded. "Then we must take our own measures to see to the poor brute. His fellow will take no harm if we turn him loose in this field until his master comes to his senses. But this one needs warmth and proper attention. How far to the nearest posting inn?"

"Matter o' seven mile, your honour," the post-boy told him.

Damon shook his head. "He'd never make it," he decided. "Any one hereabouts — some farmer perhaps — with a stable or barn where he could lie snug?"

The boy's rather sulky face brightened considerably. "*That* there is," he exclaimed quite eagerly. "Not a quarter of a mile away — and him my own uncle and as good a man as ever twanged. I'll go bail for it he'll be glad to oblige yer honour. If miss, here, will agree to it, I'll take him now, across the fields and see him safely bestowed."

'Miss' nodded vigorous approval of this suggestion, begging him only to wait till she could find her purse so that she could give him money to defray such expenses as his uncle might incur on the patient's behalf.

"By no means, ma'am," interposed Damon coolly. "This is *my* patient so it is my privilege to act the good Samaritan." He was already slipping some coins into the boy's ready palm and agreeing to Judd's suggestion that he should go along to lend a hand with bedding the patient down and to make sure the bandage did not slip. "We are already so late that another hour can make small difference," he ended resignedly, and watched the little procession set out at snail's pace across the fields, the loose horse accompanying them in an inquisitive way as though wondering what they were doing with his stable companion.

A soft voice at his side said penitently, "Now I am *truly* sorry that you should have been delayed. It is all my fault, allowing myself to be taken in by that horrid drunken wretch." She scowled darkly at the sleeper and said defensively, "But how was I to guess? I have never seen a gentleman in his cups before. I did not know *that* was how they behaved."

He could not help smiling a little. "Then you are fortunate in your first experience, ma'am. Gentlemen in their cups usually give a good deal more trouble than this one. And in causing you to seek assistance, at least he did his horse a good turn. If Judd had not noticed its condition the poor creature would certainly have bled to death. Which reminds me — I believe I have you to thank for the provision of the bandage that turned the trick. You must permit me to reimburse you for that."

"Indeed, no," she said indignantly. "You have already paid the farmer. Am I to have no share at all in the satisfaction? As for the linen I can easily buy more when I reach London. Very likely of a finer quality, too, which will please Papa, because if he *has* one tiny vanity it is his pleasure in fine linen. He dearly loves horses, too, so I daresay he will consider that his new shirts were sacrificed in a good cause."

He looked at her curiously, mildly amused by her candid remarks about her father. She was a little older than he had first thought. He had been misled, he decided, by the mouth. Her two front teeth were very slightly crossed and this gave to her upper lip an innocent childish fullness. A very kissable mouth, decided Damon impersonally. The rest of the damsel was no more than ordinarily pleasant looking. But her bearing had a confidence, her figure a rounded suppleness that suggested she was definitely out of the schoolroom. She might be eighteen and despite his first impression she was demonstrably a lady. Perhaps she, too, had been overset by the strain of a near accident, he thought charitably. Her modest travelling dress bore out her claim to social insignificance. At the moment it was sadly soiled and stained, but this she did not seem to have noticed. He wondered whither she was bound and if he ought to draw her attention to the fact that she was scarcely in a fit state to go visiting. The portmanteaux seemed to indicate a projected stay of some duration. He could not help picturing the reactions of a conventional hostess faced with such a guest.

The lady had turned her attention to the sleeping curricle driver. "What should we do about him?" she enquired hopefully, plainly expecting Damon to accept this responsibility along with the rest. "Of course he has behaved very badly, but we can scarcely leave him lying by the roadside, can we?"

Damon's mouth twitched but he hastily controlled it. "No, indeed. It makes the place look so untidy doesn't it? How shall we dispose of him?"

She eyes him suspiciously. "This is no time for funning, milord," she told him severely. "If it were to come on to rain I daresay he would take a shocking cold."

"Very probably," agreed Damon solemnly. "And a cold can be so dangerous. It might settle on his lungs and carry him off, and *then* how should we feel? But before we do anything rash, may I remind you that we don't know who he is or where he lives and that by removing him from this admittedly draughty roadside and bearing him off with us we may be subjecting his relatives to considerable anxiety. Not to mention laying ourselves open to a charge of abduction," he concluded, his sense of the ridiculous getting the better of him at last.

"I wish you will be sensible, milord," she repeated, her own lips quivering into laughter. "Perhaps he carries a pocket book or some letter which might furnish us with his direction. If you were to go through his pockets" — The brown eyes regarded him with a hint of mischief in their depths.

"And add highway robbery to the charge of abduction?" queried Damon, laughing outright. "You are determined to get me hung or at least transported, aren't you, ma'am? And let me inform you that there is something very distasteful about the notion of going through a man's pockets, however charitable one's motive."

The girl's face crumpled into mischievous laughter. She looked quite enchantingly different. "But for *me* to do so would be quite improper, as well as distasteful," she pointed out demurely.

"Very well, ma'am. But if I am taken up by the law I shall rely upon you to give evidence in my behalf — or at least to visit me in jail," he told her lightly, and stooped over the happy sleeper. Before, however, he could place himself in any danger of apprehension by the law, the sound of wheels caused him to look up. A farm tumbrel was coming down the road towards them. He rose to his feet, meaning to signal to the waggoner to stop, but this was unnecessary. The tumbrel was already creaking to a halt.

Its driver climbed down and approached him, surveying the scene of disaster with absorbed interest. Presently he announced, "That be young Master Ralph you got there." He tried to squint round Damon's tall form which chanced to come between him and the recumbent youth, gave up the attempt, and added sapiently, "Leastways that be one o' Squoire's match bays grazing in field yonder. What be come o' t'other one? And be 'e 'urt bad? Master Ralph?"

"Have you come in search of him?" asked Damon, rather amused by the newcomer's verbal economy.

"Ye might say so," drawled the carter equably. "Though 't were a load o' turnips as I come arter. But Squoire said to keep an eye lifting for 'e. Rackoned 'e'd come to grief."

"His father?" enquired Damon, interested in so Roman an approach to a son's welfare.

The carter nodded, and stumped across to gaze with mild admiration at the sleeper. "We-ell-a-well!" he exclaimed. "Squoire said 'e was cupshotten when 'e set out. Got a proper skinful now, ain't 'e? Reg'lar put about Squoire'll be."

Between them, Damon not having witnessed the actual spill, the pair explained the circumstances that had led to the young man's downfall. The carter nodded affably and said that if the gentleman wouldn't mind lending a hand to lift the sufferer into the cart he'd see about getting him home and sending a groom over to look to the horses. Squoire, he added, would reckon himself much obliged to them, specially in the matter of the bay colt, and would likely want to pay his respects.

Damon said that they must push on to London now that their help was no longer needed, whereupon the carter, obviously feeling that his master's courtesy had been adequately upheld, relapsed into bucolic serenity, tugged politely at his forelock, and set the sturdy mare in motion.

"I fancy it is not the first time that Master Ralph has returned to the ancestral halls in less lordly fashion than he set out," said Damon.

"No," agreed his fellow Samaritan. "I am sorry for his horses. Do you *really* think the colt will recover? That gash looked shockingly deep to me."

"No reason why he shouldn't," said Damon hearteningly. "He'll be scarred, of course" — and stopped abruptly at that fatal word.

But his companion was no longer listening. She was holding out one hand upon which several drops of rain had just fallen. "Pray hold me

22

excused, my lord," she said hurriedly. "I must go back to the chaise at once." And broke into a run, pulling up the hood of her loose travelling mantle as she did so.

Damon followed at a more leisurely pace, grinning at the inconsistency of the fair sex. The girl had been cool and sensible over handling a frightened wounded animal, yet fled in dismay at the prospect of a wetting.

The rain was now falling steadily. The lady who had been struggling with the portmanteaux was hurriedly replacing them in the chaise. The girl had sought shelter, but she peeped out at him as he handed up the last of the baggage.

"Thank you so much," she said. "Do, pray, step inside until this rain stops. The thing is, you see, Mama and Susan curled my hair very carefully so that Aunt Maria shouldn't give way to complete despair at the first sight of me. And if I get it wet it will be quite straight again in no time."

He had not accepted the invitation to shelter but stood leaning on the door of the chaise studying the face so confidingly turned to his, a humorous quirk to his mouth as he said gently, "Then perhaps I should also draw your attention to the state of your gown. I fear — er — Aunt Maria might take exception to that, too."

The girl cast a startled glance at her soiled grey gown and gave a little exclamation of dismay. "Oh! Barbie! What *shall* I do?"

Her companion examined the damage with grave concern. "You will have to change it, my love. Such a pity, for you have nothing else so smart. But not for the world would I have you present yourself in Berkeley Square in such a state. Perhaps the brown merino," she went on doubtfully, "though skirts are worn longer now and trimmings are quite out — unless they are made of straw." She stopped, recalling the presence of a stranger.

The stranger was listening with unaffected interest. If these two innocents imagined that the grey gown was in any sense fashionable they were sadly mistaken. The mention of Berkeley Square intrigued him, scarcely adding substance to the girl's claim of insignificance, but perhaps she was a poor relation whom 'Aunt Maria' planned to launch into society with a view to establishing her creditably. He began to feel a little sorry for the wench. She might be impertinent, quick-tempered and lacking in proper conduct, but she wasn't a bad sort of girl and had shown up well in emergency.

"And we are so late already," she was saying. "If we stop at an inn for me to change my gown it will be quite dark before we reach Town. I daresay it will cost a good deal, too."

Damon glanced round the post-chaise. To his knowledgeable eye it was plainly a hired vehicle, reasonably clean and comfortable but quite devoid of such refinements as curtains. "If I may make a suggestion," he said courteously, "my coach, with the curtains drawn, would make an adequate tiring room. The rain has stopped. If you care for the scheme, the coach is at your service and the change of costume could be effected while you wait."

Both ladies hesitated. It was a sensible suggestion and extremely kind of the gentleman. But the older lady felt that it savoured of impropriety and the younger one was oddly disinclined to accept a favour from one whom she had already designated in her own mind as 'His Arrogance'. Their glances met — enquiry, doubt, pride, mingled. Never was such a transparent pair.

He said smoothly, "Since the damage was done while Miss" — he tilted his head enquiringly.

"Forester," said the girl. "And this is my companion, Miss Hetherstone." She had almost said governess. But that would be to assent to his placing of her in the schoolgirl category, and any way Barbie was Sue's governess, had been this year past.

"My name is Skirlaugh," bowed his lordship. "If you had not come to my aid, Miss Forester, you would not have spoiled your dress. Nor would that unfortunate animal be in such good case. It would ease my conscience a good deal if you would accept this trivial service by way of amends."

The atmosphere definitely mellowed. Miss Hetherstone decided that he was most truly a gentleman. Miss Forester was softened by his tribute to her assistance. The exchange of vehicles was quickly effected while the rain obligingly held off. His lordship, keeping guard quite unnecessarily until the ladies emerged from the al fresco dressing room, decided that the brown merino, if not actually a disaster, put him strongly in mind of some ageing spinster engaged upon a mission of charity. Having expected nothing better he accepted it with fortitude, though his withers were, briefly, wrung for Aunt Maria.

Politely he ascertained Miss Forester's exact direction in Berkeley Square and asked if he might do himself the honour of calling upon Mrs.

Newton to enquire how her niece did after the unexpected rigours of her journey.

It was only when he had returned thankfully to the comfort and privacy of his own carriage that it occurred to him. These two chance-met females must have seen his disfiguring scars. Yet neither had displayed shock or disgust. Much could be set down to good breeding. But if the rest of his world treated him with a matching indifference, existence might be bearable after all. Certainly it was with a slight lifting of his spirits that he told Judd to "put 'em along a bit."

Chapter Three

Aunt Maria had begun to grow quite anxious by the time the travellers at last presented themselves in Berkeley Square. She greeted them warmly, voluble in her relief that she would not now have to put dinner back, since nothing annoyed Uncle Matthew more, and concealing her dismay at the brown merino and the limp, crushed curls. "I was sorry to have missed you when your uncle and I paid such a very hurried visit to your dear parents last month," she said kindly. "Your mama said you were visiting friends in Westerham. But it was the only day that your uncle could spare to go with me, so occupied as he has been ever since the peace negotiations began. I am sure we are all heartily glad that the war is over at last, but your poor uncle is kept busier than ever. Something to do with the rights of those dreadful colonists to fish off Newfoundland — though what that has to do with the war *or* the peace I'm sure no one could imagine. But there! There's no understanding politics anyway, and I don't know why I am boring on about such dull matters when I expect you are all agog to hear about my plans for introducing you into society."

"Papa says that the fishing rights are just a sop to satisfy the Northern States," offered Alethea obligingly. "The really important issues are the Western Territories and the Canadian frontier."

Aunt Maria looked horrified. "My dear child! What can you possibly know about such things? I *do* hope you aren't *blue*! It would be quite fatal I assure you. Young ladies are not expected to understand affairs of state, far less to speak of them with such confidence. Should you chance to fall into conversation with a gentleman who is interested in serious matters — which is most unlikely, since the younger gentlemen care only for sport or, perhaps, for the set of a coat or the nice arrangement of a neckcloth — then a pretty diffidence, an air of reverence for the greater understanding of the superior sex, is all that will be required of you. In this respect I would advise you to study your cousin. I daresay I am over partial, being her mama, but it is only simple truth to acknowledge that she has any number of admirers, of the highest 'ton'. And *she* hasn't the least notion of politics. So you see!"

At this point Miss Hetherstone hurriedly intervened, explaining that Mr. Forester had been deeply interested in the constitutional struggle so recently terminated, and had, in his own enthusiasm, carried his daughter perhaps a little out of her depth. "But I am sure, ma'am, that she would never put herself forward unbecomingly," she added firmly.

Aunt Maria smiled indulgently. "I see that I shall have to show you how to go on," she said. "A débutante in her first season must be *so* careful; her behaviour modest, without gaucherie; her dress exquisite but simple — white for evenings, of course — no vivid colours or extravagance of style."

"Oh dear!" said her niece in accents of dismay. "*Must* it be white?"

"For your come-out, most certainly. Pale colours are permissible on other occasions. But until you have been given vouchers for Almack's you cannot be too discreet. And one can never take that privilege for granted. Indeed I was in agonies lest Tina should be refused them last year. That dreadful riding habit that she bought, quite unknown to me! Quite wickedly becoming, of course, but *most* improper. Kit said even the horse was shocked. It tried to bolt with her. Just funning, you know. That is Kit Grayson — they are childhood friends. So fortunate that he was riding in the Park and was able to prevent an accident, though it would have been more useful if he had been able to dissuade her from choosing so unreliable a mount just because it matched her hair. But if she had been *seen*! Oh yes! Most certainly it must be white."

Alethea, who had been trying to reconcile this somewhat elliptical account of her cousin's conduct with Aunt Maria's suggestion that she should model her own upon it, blinked at her in amazement, having quite lost track of the original argument. But Aunt Maria was already off again.

"I mean to give a small ball to introduce you into society. Rather a sober affair, I am afraid. But since you have no acquaintance in Town I judged it best to invite family parties — the members of my own intimate circle with their sons and daughters. As soon as you are suitably dressed I shall begin to take you about with me in a quiet sort of way — morning visits, you know, and walking in the Park. Perhaps one or two concerts and theatres, so that you will get to know people gradually and will not feel yourself surrounded by strangers when the time comes for your formal début. But the first thing is to buy you one or two dresses, for the one you are wearing" — she could restrain herself no longer — "is quite deplorable."

Alethea looked guilty. She did not know quite how it had come about, but it so chanced that neither she nor Miss Hetherstone had mentioned the change of costume that had taken place on the way to Town. They had naturally spoken of the accident which was responsible for their tardy arrival, but somehow that final chapter of the story had not emerged. It was very easy, Alethea was already discovering, to keep silence on delicate subjects and permit Aunt Maria to do the talking. She seemed to have an inexhaustible flow of conversation that covered any awkward pauses. In any case, the grey travelling dress that had been so hastily bundled back into the portmanteau was hardly more likely to have earned her approval than the brown one. Both had been made by a village dressmaker with more regard to durability than to the dictates of fashion.

"Mama decided it would be foolish to have dresses made at home," she said meekly. "Better to wait till I reached Town where I should have the benefit of your advice. She said I was a very lucky girl because you had such exquisite taste," she added, half hoping that the compliment might soften her aunt's attitude about white as the only possible colour for a débutante's ball gown.

Aunt Maria accepted it as no more than her due. "I have always had an eye for line and colour," she agreed complacently. "But in this case it is not so much a matter of choosing what best becomes you as of dressing you in the accepted mode. Not but what your dresses will be pretty as well," she encouraged. "Nothing, to be sure, could be quite as bad as *that*." She nodded at the brown merino. "And I must say you are improved in looks since last I saw you. I don't at all despair of being able to present you quite creditably."

"But not in white," said Alethea mournfully. "It makes me look haggard and sickly."

Miss Hetherstone plucked up courage to add her timid protest to her charge's. "Do not young girls sometimes wear pale pink or blue?" she ventured. "Alethea looks quite charmingly in pink."

Mrs. Newton frowned. That was probably true, she thought. Her niece had the creamy skin that so often went with brown eyes and hair, a skin that was clear and smooth but lacked colour. The warmer tints which would lend a glow would undoubtedly be the most becoming to her. It was true, too, that many young girls wore pale colours. Unfortunately Tina, unlike most red-heads, looked quite ravishingly lovely in delicate shades of pink and wore them frequently. So it was manifestly impossible to permit Alethea to do so. Tina would be quite sufficiently displeased by the improvement in the girl's looks since their last meeting. Alethea, then, had been a thin, solemn-eyed sixteen-year-old. Even now, no one was going to acclaim her as an undoubted beauty, but she had grown into quite a taking little thing, with a pretty smile and a really delicious figure — even in that hideous merino. To dress her in pink would undoubtedly provoke one of Tina's worst tantrums. The very thought of it caused her parent to shudder violently, a manifestation that her respectful audience not unnaturally attributed to shock at their ignorant presumption.

Alethea sighed and abandoned the dream of a slender brown-haired girl in a shell-pink ball gown. "I didn't mean to tease you, aunt," she said penitently. "I will wear white if you think it best."

Such prompt docility was quite foreign to Aunt Maria's experience. "Dear child!" she murmured. "Always so sensible and so biddable! Clement and Verona are greatly blessed in their children. I was very happy to see Susan so careful of your dear Mama. And what is more, she bids fair to be quite charmingly pretty in a year or two. Which is a fortunate circumstance, since *she* can scarcely look to inherit a fortune as you did. But there! Your parents most particularly asked me not to speak of your circumstances and here I am running on about them already! Though I daresay it doesn't signify, since it is all in the family," she concluded, smiling very kindly at Miss Hetherstone.

"Susan will have quite a respectable portion," said Alethea composedly. "When Papa explained that it was not within my power to share my inheritance with her, Mama and I put our heads together and agreed that since I was so amply provided for, it was only right that Mama's money should all be settled on Sue instead of being divided between us as was her first intention."

If Aunt Maria was startled at the notion of parents openly discussing such arrangements with their children, she was at least confirmed in her good opinion of her niece's principles. Her eyes actually misted with sentimental tears, and she said impulsively, "You know, my love, I have been thinking that a soft shade of *cream* might be the thing for your ball dress. Not so harsh as dead white, yet quite acceptable, even to the highest sticklers. I have just the very shade in mind — the colour of cream that has set in the pan and shows golden in the folds as it wrinkles under the skimmer."

This vivid word picture awoke enthusiasm in her listeners. When she went on to speak of a ruched overdress, its flounces caught up with knots of ribbon or tiny posies — perhaps cherry coloured — Alethea's eyes shone, and the speaker was obviously carried away by her own creative artistry.

"Cherry colour is rather daring, of course," she pondered happily, "but permissible, I think, if used with discretion." And then stopped short, her mouth a little open, on her face an expression of arrested dismay. Her audience waited anxiously. Presently she said slowly, "But I don't know if it will serve. A good deal depends on what Tina wishes to wear. If she chooses the green gauze, then cherry will do very well. But if it is the pink sarsenet" — she broke off, pleating her handkerchief between her fingers in nervous embarrassment; then said on a placatory note, "She is in her second season, you see, and so she may wear colours. And since she will be helping us to receive the guests it will not do for your gowns to clash. We will decide on cream for the dress, but cherry colour" —

The door of the saloon was roughly flung open. Miss Tina Newton whirled gaily into the room. Miss Hetherstone's lips primmed in unconscious rebuke of the unceremonious arrival. Alethea glanced up eagerly, admiration writ plain in her expression. But Miss Newton did not appear to notice that her mama was not alone.

"Mama, Mama!" she exclaimed impetuously. "The most wonderful thing! You will never guess what I have just heard. Oh! It is beyond anything great. You must send to Madame Denise at once. I simply must have the new lilac silk for next Thursday's theatre party. And I shall wear your amethyst set with it. Now don't be saying it is too old for me, for I mean only to wear the necklet and *one* of the bracelets, and they, I am sure, will be just the thing. Especially the necklet, since *you* said the gown was cut too low."

"My dear child," said Mrs. Newton in tones of fond reproof. "What can you be thinking of? Do you not see that we have visitors? Here is your cousin arrived this hour past, and you not here to welcome her. And I do not think you have met Miss Hetherstone before."

The animation faded from Tina's face but she acknowledged the introduction politely and apologised for her casual behaviour, turning to Alethea to add, "And since my cousin is come to join our family I am sure she would not wish me to stand on ceremony. So stuffy and uncomfortable! The thing is, I had just learned that an old friend is back in Town and in my excitement I forgot everything else. Would you not like me to show you to your room so that you may change your travelling dress?" Her eyes ran thoughtfully over the brown merino. "I daresay Hetty will have unpacked for you by now. Mama, you *did* say Hetty was to wait upon my cousin, did you not?"

Mrs. Newton assented, and said that she herself would escort Miss Hetherstone to her room as she knew that the cousins must be longing to exchange girlish secrets.

If this was in fact the case, both young ladies showed commendable restraint, though Tina did, indeed, smother a giggle as they climbed the stairs, and to Alethea's enquiring glance said lightly, "You served me well there, cousin. I have been trying to escape from Hetty's watchful eye these six months past. In Town, you know, one mustn't set foot out of doors without a maid or a chaperone in attendance. And Hetty is too vigilant by half. I can't so much as say good morning to a gentleman in the Park but she must enquire into his respectability and wish to know where I met him. While as for exchanging a few harmless remarks in the library while I am choosing Mama's books, she rings such a peal over me that you would think I was planning an elopement at the least. The trouble is that she was my nurse before she was my maid and she behaves as though I was still a child. But I don't suppose she'll put herself about over you. In any case you've no acquaintance in Town so it wouldn't matter."

The light contemptuous tone rankled. Only the recollection that she was a guest in her aunt's house kept Alethea from unbecoming retort, so she was not particularly surprised to discover that the middle-aged abigail who awaited her bore no resemblance to the dragon of Tina's description. She was a buxom, fresh-complexioned creature with pleasant grey eyes and a friendly smile who welcomed the stranger kindly and said that miss's dotted muslin would be ready in a minute. She had begged Hebe, madam's own maid to press it out for her, so crumpled as it was, and she herself anxious to finish the unpacking. "And who did your packing for you, miss, I can't imagine," she added severely. "As well have stirred your portmanteaux with a soup ladle. Never did I see such a mixter-maxter. While as for this" — she held up a stained grey dress — "I doubt if even I can make it wearable. Not but what" — she broke off in some confusion.

"Not but what it would be no great loss?" suggested Alethea, laughing. "You are very right! All my dresses are old fashioned. But Aunt Maria is to buy me an entire new wardrobe. So you may throw that one away with my very good will."

Hetty looked suitably shocked at such reckless extravagance though she was privately of the opinion that most of the dresses she had unpacked deserved no better treatment. She was curious, too, to discover the tale that lay behind the hasty, inexpert packing and a bloodstained gown. She eyed Miss Forester's candid, laughing countenance and ventured to probe the mystery a little further.

"It's a blessing those stains haven't marked any of your other things," she commented, "seeing as they're still quite wet."

Miss Tina would have snubbed her sharply at that point or ignored the remark completely. Miss Alethea only laughed, agreed that it was a good thing she hadn't been wearing a gown that she was particularly fond of when the accident occurred, and poured out the whole story. Or most of it. If Hetty never learned exactly where the change of costume had taken place, it was doubtless because Hebe came in with the freshly pressed muslin and had to be thanked for her kindness. By the time that she had helped her new charge into her simple evening gown, Hetty's first impressions were favourable. No beauty, but pleasant ways and good manners. Brushing out the fine silky hair, she volunteered the information that she remembered Miss Alethea's mama as a young girl, not yet out.

"Very kind she was to me," she explained. "It was my first place and me just thirteen. I was so homesick I cried myself to sleep every night. But then the mistress — your grandmama that was — said I should wait on the schoolroom. And Miss Verona and Miss Maria used to joke me and make me laugh and give me ribbons and sugar sticks and a kitten to cuddle up in bed. Never was two nicer young ladies. You put me in mind of Miss Verona with your way of talking, though you're not like her in looks."

There was a rueful twinkle in Alethea's eyes. "No, alas! Susan is the one who takes after Mama. I am said to resemble Papa's sister, but since she died before I was born I cannot venture an opinion on that. Both Mama and Aunt Maria were acknowledged beauties, were they not? And my cousin Tina is the loveliest creature imaginable. I am sure she shines all the others down at the 'ton' parties. It is really very disheartening." But the cheerful voice belied the doleful words. Growing up with a pretty sister, even if Susan would never compare with the exquisite Tina, Alethea was well accustomed to the knowledge that she had no claim to beauty.

"Handsome is as handsome does," retorted Hetty tartly. "For my part, if I were a gentleman, I'd rather settle for a good disposition than a pretty face."

"So Papa was used to say," said Alethea demurely, a dimple peeping and her straight little nose wrinkling mischievously. "*He* said I should study to make myself agreeable and helpful, and to mend my temper which is inclined to be hasty. But it would be so much easier just to be naturally beautiful without any effort, wouldn't it?"

"Go along with you, miss," said Hetty capitulating entirely. "Your Papa's in the right of it as maybe you'll find out some day. Now can you find your own way downstairs or would you wish me to show you?"

Tina, meanwhile, having left her cousin with Hetty, had hurried to her mother's dressing room. Since kindly Mrs. Newton had lingered to assure herself that every attention had been paid to the comfort of even so insignificant a guest as Miss Hetherstone, she had some minutes to wait, and by the time that her mama at last hurried in she was fuming with impatience.

"What *have* you been doing Mama? You must have known I wanted private speech with you and that the matter was urgent. Send Hebe away."

"But my love!" remonstrated Mrs. Newton, glancing anxiously at the dainty Louis Quinze clock that stood on the mantel shelf. "It lacks but half an hour to dinner. I shall never be ready in time. And your cousin's first night with us. Can it not wait?"

"No. And by the looks of her, my cousin wouldn't know the difference if you came down to dinner in your bedgown."

Mrs. Newton nodded resignedly to Hebe, who went out of the room with something suspiciously like a flounce.

"But do, pray, make haste, my love," she urged. "You know how unpunctuality annoys Papa."

Tina's eyes were huge and dark with barely suppressed excitement. "It is Skirlaugh, Mama. He is back in Town at last. I had it from Kit Grayson. Skirlaugh is to dine with him tonight. I want you to send him a card for my cousin's party."

Chapter Four

No argument would persuade Tina that it was quite impossible for any self-respecting parent to submit to her demand. Invite a gentleman whom she had never met to her party? And to a party so intimate and so important as a coming-out? No lady of principle would do so. The fact that the gentleman was heir to a duke only made matters worse. It would be to incur accusations of tuft-hunting and toad-eating, even from her friends. Worse! They might even suspect her of trying to entrap such an eligible matrimonial prize for her daughter's benefit. Had Tina not thought of that?

Tina had. It was, she coolly announced, the very object that she had in mind. Did not Mama think that she would make a delightful duchess? As for never having met Lord Skirlaugh, did Mama not recall that he had been present at the ball that the Graysons had given for Marianne?

"But *I* did not *go* to the ball," moaned her afflicted parent. "And I wish I had not permitted *you* to attend, and you only sixteen. Only they were old friends and close neighbours and you teased me so."

Tina smiled. "As I shall tease you again, dear Mama," she promised sweetly. "He was not particularly eligible then," she explained kindly. "His brother was still alive. And married. Nor did he pay me a great deal of attention, being still besotted about Elinor Coutance. She jilted him, you know, when the brother's son was born. How she must regret it now! I believe she eventually married a mere nobody. Wealthy, of course, but what is the use of wealth alone when one wishes to cut a figure in the world?"

Thinking of a daughter's dress bills, Mrs. Newton might have said that it was a good deal of use. But the clock, at that minute chiming the quarter, she rang for Hebe, saying that it could serve no useful purpose to set Papa all on end by being late for dinner, and shooed her daughter away to her own hurried toilet.

Dinner began uncomfortably. Uncle Matthew was a trifle out of temper during the first course, glancing pointedly at the clock when his wife hurried downstairs and irritably enquiring the reason when his daughter made her even later appearance.

"Hetty had to wait on my cousin first," explained that young lady with aplomb.

"And Alethea's arrival was delayed," supplemented Mrs. Newton swiftly, and launched into an animated account of the incident which had caused the trouble.

By the time that she had dealt faithfully with this absorbing tale her spouse was sufficiently mollified by the succulence of a portion of duck that he was consuming and the smoothness of the burgundy that accompanied it to remember his duties as host. He addressed one or two civil remarks to Miss Hetherstone, charging her with several messages for her employers and expressing the hope that her return journey would not be marred by any such unfortunate incident as had caused today's delay. He then turned his attention to his niece, hoped that she would be comfortable under his roof and said he had no doubt she was longing to sample the attractions of London's shops, coupled with a playful warning not to draw the bustle too freely.

Alethea assured him that she had been bred to habits of economy and would, moreover, have her aunt's guidance to check any foolish extravagance. That provoked a slightly satirical smile, but he listened kindly enough as she told him how eagerly she had looked forward to this visit and how much she longed to see the famous and beautiful buildings which her father had described as being steeped in history. When the ladies rose to leave him to his wine he actually patted her hand and told her that she seemed to be a sensible little thing and not wholly given over to fashionable frivolities, a remark which his daughter took in bad part.

"Doing it a little too brown, cousin," she said coldly, as they followed the two older ladies into the drawing room. "Your enthusiasm for a lot of mouldering old bones and stones was most affecting. Very credibly performed. But Papa is no fool. He can detect a sham with the best. So don't overplay your hand." And before Alethea, cheeks burning, could protest her sincerity, had strolled across to join her mother and very soon after announced her intention of going early to bed as she had the headache.

The week that followed gave Alethea little time for brooding over Tina's unkindness and none at all for sightseeing. Aunt Maria, having looked over her niece's wardrobe, decreed an immediate visit to Bond Street.

"One or two dresses for day wear and another muslin for evenings you must have at once. I am not, in general, an advocate of such hurried buying, but to be honest, my love, you have nothing fit for Town wear. Then Denise shall measure you for the rest."

The orgy of shopping that followed was sheer intoxication. As a schoolgirl Alethea had been dressed with appropriate simplicity. Mama, a prudent woman, saw no sense in frittering away her limited resources on girls who had not done growing. There had followed six months of mourning for Cousin Albert. As a result, Alethea had never before bought a gown simply because it enhanced her appearance. Joyously she feasted her eyes on the rich and delicate fabrics displayed for her approval and stood patiently to be fitted while Aunt Maria and Madame Denise discussed the draping of an overskirt or the fall of a sleeve. Then there were bonnets and slippers and gloves to be chosen and even petticoats of gauze and Indian muslin for evening wear, though Aunt Maria had conceded that her own linen shifts and petticoats would do very well for every day.

Remembering her uncle's warning, Alethea rather timidly questioned the cost of all this finery, for nothing so vulgar as price was ever mentioned. Aunt Maria only laughed and told her not to trouble her head. It might be better, she decided, to ask Uncle Matthew how matters stood. After all it was Uncle Matthew who held the purse strings and he would soon tell her if she was in danger of outrunning the constable. An attempt to express her gratitude to her aunt for devoting so much of her time to, "rigging me out in prime style, as brother Charles would so elegantly phrase it," met with no better success.

"Dear Charles," said Aunt Maria affectionately. "A pity that he is not here to escort you to parties. How does he go on in Vienna?"

Had she but known it, Aunt Maria was extremely grateful for the distraction provided by a task that was so much to her liking. Distraction *and* protection. For not only did she delight in choosing clothes for one so appreciative as her niece, not only was it proving to be a surprisingly rewarding task, but also, when she was with Alethea, Tina left her in peace.

For Tina was driving her mother hard. Persistently she renewed her demand that Lord Skirlaugh should be invited to Alethea's debut. And this time Mrs. Newton was determined that she would not yield. She steeled herself against tirade and coaxing alike, but it made her miserably unhappy, and only with Alethea did she feel safe from attack, since Tina never mentioned his lordship's name in front of her cousin.

Between them, unwittingly, Tina and Lord Skirlaugh served Alethea well. In indulging her excellent clothes sense to the full, Aunt Maria quite forgot that her daughter would scarcely look with approval upon garments that gave the little country cousin a new and unexpectedly charming touch. She threw caution to the winds. Alethea's coming-out dress was almost finished. It was fashioned in the bergère style made popular by the French queen and Mrs. Newton had chosen for its creation a heavy silk damask, the cost of which would have supported a genuine shepherdess in considerable comfort for several years. Now, in a sudden access of decision, she decreed that its flounces should be caught up with tiny posies of red rosebuds tied with matching velvet ribbon.

Alethea brooded happily over the thought of the lovely thing as she sat sewing beside the drawing room fire. She and Aunt Maria were to sup quietly together, since Uncle Matthew was gone to Somerset House to a meeting of the Royal Society and this was the night of Tina's theatre party. She was beginning, she decided, to understand Aunt Maria's insistence on the importance of line, colour and cut, her scorn of meretricious ornament. In some inexplicable way the bergère gown lent its wearer a suggestion of added height and poise that made all the difference to her confidence. And at that moment, as if in striking demonstration of her mama's theory, Tina came swiftly into the room wearing the new lilac silk. She had dressed early, since she was engaged to dine with the Graysons, whose party it was, and she had dressed in haste, since she had returned late from an expedition to the Botanic Gardens in Chelsea, an expedition which Alethea suspected to be merely a cover for some assignation which Aunt Maria would not approve, since she could not imagine Tina nourishing a serious interest in herbs and simples.

Perhaps it was the excitement of a secret flirtation that had put the delicate glow in her cheek, the mischievous curve to her lips, but not even the scrambling haste in which she had dressed could mar the perfection of Madame Denise's creation. Yet the dress was severely plain, save for the foam of ruffles that fell away from the elbows to focus attention on slim white arms and dimpled hands. The great amethyst which glimmered at her throat was a perfect match for the silk. It was only her own rustic ignorance, decided Alethea, that gave her the uneasy feeling that the whole effect was a little too grand for the occasion, a little too old for its wearer.

Aunt Maria exclaimed in delight and began to examine and praise the gown in detail, but for once Tina was in no mood for compliments and shrugged them aside brusquely.

"Very true, Mama. So I am in my best looks — as my mirror has already told me. Of more import, have you sent Lord Skirlaugh a card for our party yet? Since it is but ten days off you cannot in courtesy delay any longer."

Mrs. Newton's happy flutterings and pattings ceased abruptly. She made a brave attempt to assert her authority.

"I wish you will not tease me to behave so improperly," she said with dignity. "I am sure I have explained to you half a dozen times why I cannot do so. So vulgar! So coming! I am sure we may hold up our heads with the highest when it comes to breeding. We have no need to fawn upon anyone just because they chance to be of noble rank, And anyway" — coming down a little from this lofty note — "Byram is quite small — almost insignificant for a ducal seat — and his grace is by no means a rich man, while as for Lord Skirlaugh, I believe he was quite shockingly scarred in that tragic business when the baby was burnt to death. You could never endure the sight of such disfigurement — you, who sickened at the mere thought of being obliged to dance with Captain Goldthorpe who had had the misfortune to lose two fingers."

"You under-rate my fortitude, Mama," returned her daughter lightly. "As for Byram's insignificance — here's a high flight, indeed! There's not an ambitious parent in the whole of the 'ton' would agree with you. No duke can be insignificant. And if Byram's holdings do not compare with Devonshire's, his title is almost as old. As for his son's scars — he is heir to a duke and he is looking about him for a wife. Which two circumstances, dear Mama, would reconcile me to a degree of disfigurement that would surprise you!"

At the first mention of Lord Skirlaugh's name Alethea's lips had parted. Had opportunity served she would have mentioned her own slight acquaintance with his lordship, have assured her relatives that there was nothing in his appearance to disgust any reasonable person. But in the heat of their argument they had forgotten her presence. Short of interrupting them with downright rudeness it was impossible to intervene, and by the time that Tina had done speaking she no longer had any desire to do so. She bent her head over her sewing — the linen for Papa's shirts had been replaced during one of her earliest shopping expeditions — and left the contestants to settle their own differences.

Tina's shameless avowal of opportunism did nothing to advance her cause. Mrs. Newton held firm, and her daughter presently stalked away to her evening's pleasuring in high dudgeon.

It was some time before Alethea could calm her aunt's distress. To have her daughter so expose herself in front of her cousin! Soothing suggestions that it was just because it *was* all in the family, that doubtless she had not meant the half of it, eventually had a beneficial effect, and a happy reference to the lilac gown, which she could praise without reserve, eventually directed the sufferer's thoughts into pleasanter channels. She dried her eyes, assured her niece that she was the greatest possible comfort, and was presently able to consume her breast of chicken cooked in white wine sauce with moderate appetite.

Worn out by excessive emotion she fell asleep in her chair after supper and Alethea was free to pursue her own thoughts. She pondered the ugly scene of which she had been an unwilling witness. It had needed only brief acquaintance to convince her that Tina was wholly self-centred and had little regard for truth, but to some extent the vivacious gaiety had blinded her to the girl's innate cold-heartedness. Even in memory she sickened a little at the callous reference to a man's disfigurement, the calculating evaluation of his matrimonial worth. So he was heir to a dukedom, was he? Perhaps that accounted for his arrogance. He had never fulfilled his promise to call in Berkeley Square, and under the circumstances she could only be glad of it. She wondered if they would meet again, and if he would recognise her in her smart new dresses. It would be awkward if he claimed acquaintance in front of her aunt. She wished she had made a clean breast of the whole story at the outset; then consoled herself with the thought that he was unlikely to notice her existence if Tina meant to make a play for him.

She was surprised to find herself feeling rather sorry for the gentleman. She had taken him in dislike at first meeting but he had turned out to be quite a useful sort of man after all. Too good for Tina's machinations, anyway. She hoped he was able to look after himself but doubted if any man could resist her cousin when she set herself out to please. With a little sigh she began to fold up her work.

The tea tray was brought in and Aunt Maria had just announced her intention of retiring early — largely, Alethea suspected, in order to avoid another unpleasant encounter with her daughter — when that young lady herself walked in. Aunt Maria looked up apprehensively, but Tina was now, apparently, in the sunniest of humours.

The evening had been perfectly delightful. No, she couldn't recall the name of the piece. She rather thought it had been something of Sheridan's. Or was it Shakespeare? Anyway, everyone was in raptures over it. But her own party had not stayed to see the last act. Mrs. Grayson had been sadly affected by the heat and had to be taken home. Oh, yes — she was perfectly recovered. It was just the heat, and the crush of visitors to their box. It seemed as though everyone they knew had come to exchange greetings with them.

She was a good deal better informed about the audience, listing in considerable detail all the notable members of the 'ton' who had been present, together with descriptions of the toilets and jewels worn by the ladies. Her own gown had been vastly admired. And was the tea still hot, because she was thirsty and would like some.

While Aunt Maria rang for fresh tea, Alethea studied her cousin curiously. How did one reconcile the fury of her departure with this present amiability? Had she been so easily diverted by an evening of innocuous pleasure? Alethea did not think so. There was an air of scarce-contained satisfaction about her as she sat sipping her tea and retailing the various compliments that had been paid her. Taken in conjunction with her tawny colouring it put Althea strongly in mind of a tigress, full fed, an impression that was strengthened when she put down her cup and got to her feet, yawning unashamedly, with a display of strong white teeth.

"I am for bed," she told them. "I am riding with Kit tomorrow, early. Oh, yes! That reminds me. He brought Skirlaugh to our box during the second interval. He remembered me perfectly well from Marianne's party. So I begged him to come to my cousin's — said you would certainly have sent him a card for it if you had known he was in Town and that Kit was already promised to attend. He made the usual polite protestations about not wishing to take advantage of your hospitality, but I told him you were never one to stand on ceremony and that it was to be quite an informal affair. And the long and the short of it is that he said he would be happy to accept."

Chapter Five

Aunt Maria succumbed to one of her worst spasms and took to her bed. She could not, she moaned piteously, endure the sympathetic murmurs of her friends, the malicious laughter of her enemies when the tale was spread abroad. As spread it would inevitably be since the incident had occurred in such a public place. Little wonder that poor Mrs. Grayson had felt herself so overcome that she had asked to be taken home. The consequences of Tina's malapert behaviour would be far-reaching and unpleasant. And to have described her cousin's coming-out party as 'quite an informal affair' — the sort of function to which anyone could be given a casual last minute invitation! And that in the hearing of several highly interested bystanders.

When Aunt Maria remembered the meticulous care with which she had drawn up her list of guests to ensure that her niece should have the best possible start in her social career, she wept anew. What would they think — those awe-inspiring dowagers, those younger but still haughty ladies whose approval was so necessary to any aspiring débutante?

Tina laughed and said it was all nonsense. The arbiters of fashion were too consequential by half. A good set-down would do most of them a world of good. And if they criticised her conduct it was only because they were as mad as fire because she had stolen a march on them. Lord Skirlaugh had not yet put in any appearance at private parties. In securing his promise of attendance she had achieved a social triumph and Mama should really be grateful to her. She went off without a care in the world to keep her riding engagement next day and, in general, went about as usual, coaxing Mrs. Grayson into chaperoning her when it was essential and leaving attendance on her mother to her cousin and the servants.

She stopped laughing when the physician called in to prescribe for her prostrated parent spoke of a shattered nervous system, stressed the need for rest and advised withdrawal to some quiet watering place. What! Permit Mama to leave Town just now? Perhaps be constrained to go with her? Impossible!

After careful thought and a hurried shopping expedition she descended upon the sick room and was so fortunate as to find her mother alone. She

41

had just fallen into a light doze and Hebe had slipped downstairs to snatch a belated luncheon. Tina proceeded to make up the fire with quite unnecessary energy and a good deal of noise. Having successfully awakened the sleeper she bent to drop a light kiss on her cheek, seated herself in the chair beside the bed and opened her campaign.

"Dear Mama," she murmured sweetly. "And looking so *very* much better. I really ought to scold you, you know, causing us so much anxiety, and all through wearing yourself out in dancing attendance on my tiresome cousin."

Mama attempted a feeble protest at this distorted version of the case but was gently overborne. "Oh! I suppose she is not really tiresome. It is just that she does not understand the delicacy of your constitution and how your brave spirit drives you to maintain a cheerful front long after you should have yielded to your exhaustion. But you must not blame me for being the tiniest bit cross with her when she has permitted my dear Mama to wear herself to the bone in this ridiculous fashion."

Mrs. Newton listened as one hypnotised. By the time that her pillows had been re-arranged so that she might try on the charming lace cap which her devoted daughter had brought to cheer her — and for which Tina had blithely pledged Mama's credit with Madame Denise — she was, if not convinced that Alethea was the cause of all her troubles, at least prepared to believe that Tina thought so. To have her daughter fussing over her, dressing her hair so that the new cap should be seen to the best advantage, assuring her that there was still scarcely a grey hair among the abundant locks but adding severely that she would be the better for a touch of rouge, so pale as she was, exercised a highly beneficial effect. When Hebe slipped soft-footed into the room she was horrified to find the invalid established on the day bed in the window bay, the curtains, which had been kept close shut these past three days, flung back to admit the spring sunshine. Dressed in her prettiest negligee of a tabby silk that combined every shade of blue from soft azure to deepest turquoise, the lappets of the new cap tied in a fetching bow beneath her chin, Mrs. Newton was listening happily while Tina told her just how well the shimmering, changing hues of the silk accentuated the blue of her eyes, vowing naughtily that the garment was far too pretty to be wasted on a mere husband and that Mama must really think about setting up a cavalier servente who would truly appreciate it.

"Made me mad enough to bust a stay-lace," the indignant Hebe told the select coterie in the housekeeper's room that night, gentility of speech

42

forgotten in her outrage. "There's Cook nearly frantic with brewing possets and sending up gruel and jellies and panadas only to have them sent down again, and me and Hetty at our wits' end to know what to try next. We bathed her temples with vinegar and lavender water. We massaged her neck and her hands and feet. We propped her up on pillows and fanned her and gave her a vinaigrette to sniff. Miss Alethea talked to her so kind and sensible she might have been a grown woman herself. And the only thing that did any good was the syrup of poppies that Dr. Philipson persuaded her to swallow. That *did* put her to sleep and gave all of us a chance to snatch some rest. But as soon as she woke up it was all to do again. Proper low she's got, poor lady, all along of Miss Tina's cantrips. And then, in walks young madam with her wheedling ways and fairly bewitches her Mama into being better. And she really *is* better, which I'm sure is a blessing, sending a message to Mrs. Grayson to come and bear her company a while this evening and vowing she'll get up tomorrow. I'm sure I'm as thankful as anyone to see her plucking up again, but that Miss Tina makes me want to spit." An inelegant avowal that was received in sympathetic silence.

Fortunately Mrs Grayson was one of Tina's admirers. Until Thursday night she had seen only that young lady's party manners. Moreover she knew that her son was deep in love with the wilful beauty and since she was almost as doting a parent as Mrs. Newton herself she would do nothing to cast a rub in his way. Carefully primed by Tina she made no mention of certain cold glances and curious stares which had been directed at her charge when she had escorted her to Almack's on the previous evening. Mama would only start fretting again, Tina had said. And while seizing the opportunity to point out to the girl the damage that had been done by her heedlessness, Mrs. Grayson was pleased to find her so thoughtful of her mother's peace of mind.

So there was nothing to hinder Mrs. Newton's complete recovery. A timely reminder from her thoughtful daughter that there was much to be done if Alethea's party was not to fall short of the degree of hospitality expected of so notable a hostess hastened her resumption of her normal activities and permitted Miss Newton to discard the boring role of ministering angel. She, too, resumed her busy social life.

But with a difference. Patiently she set herself to win over those captious critics who had shown disapproval of her boldness. If report was to be believed the Byrams were among the ranks of the high sticklers and their son was probably cut from the same cloth. His bride would be chosen to please his parents and to fit the dignity of the position that she would one day hold. So there was a new gravity in Miss Newton's expression. A gentle modesty informed her voice and bearing. She astounded two of her most virulent critics by declining — in their hearing — an invitation to make one of a party to attend a masquerade at Vauxhall Gardens, on the grounds that her Mama would not like it. The two ladies stared incredulously, but were visibly shaken. Tina maintained her demure front with some difficulty. But it was worth it. There should be no hint that she was 'rather fast', no suggestion that she was 'not quite the thing', to blemish the reputation of the young lady who meant to be the next Duchess of Byram.

Her most difficult task was preventing Kit Grayson from making her a declaration, an event which must at all costs be held off until she had secured her interest with his cousin. At present Kit was her only link with Lord Skirlaugh and she had no intention of giving him his congé while he served so useful a purpose. Unfortunately her pose of demure maiden modesty worked so powerfully upon the young man's chivalrous instincts that even *her* skilful management was tested to the limit. She was obliged to fall back on excusing herself from riding or driving with him. The claims of her Mama, still sadly frail, she explained gently, and of her cousin — so homesick and so shy, poor lamb — served as sufficient reason, while in no way diminishing the young man's adoring fervour. He perfectly understood her sentiments, could but honour her for them despite his own disappointment, and pressed a reverent kiss on her hand as he took his leave.

Tina studied his departing back thoughtfully. He would, she thought, make a very manageable husband. Wealthy, too, and so very good looking. She permitted herself a shudder of revulsion at the memory of Lord Skirlaugh's scarred face. But *he* could make her a duchess. Kit was not even a baronet. She turned to more profitable considerations. It seemed that there was a good deal to be said for the charm of girlish shyness. Certainly it had driven Kit to the point of making her an offer. Perhaps it might have a similar effect upon his cousin. She must study to improve her portrayal.

Mrs. Newton, reviewing the arrangements for her party, decided that she would add champagne to the various beverages with which she planned to refresh her guests in the intervals between dancing. The supper she had ordered could not be improved upon, but the champagne would add a note of distinction. She went off to consult her husband over the choice of wines and then to supervise the decoration of the ballroom and the gallery where the musicians would be placed. Tina, still pursuing her fancy for the charms of simplicity, went off to consult Madame Denise. One must, after all, dress the part, if one hoped to play it convincingly.

Alethea found herself with a good deal of time on her hands. A preoccupied Aunt Maria suggested that Hetty should escort her to see some of the sights of Town. So busy as they had been with one thing and another, there had been no time for sight-seeing. The suggestion was much to Alethea's taste, though Hetty was scarcely the companion she would have chosen. She was the kindest of creatures and Alethea had already grown very fond of her. As a guide for shopping expedition she was superlative, knowing just where to obtain whatever was required. But sight-seeing bored her. She had no interest in history, no respect for architectural beauty. Westminster Abbey, she said, would be all the better for a good clean. And if they couldn't afford to buy new banners to replace all those dirty, tattered rags, why didn't they, at least, wash them? The Tower of London would set off her rheumatic pains if she stayed any longer within its damp precincts, while as for the smell of the animals in the menagerie, it fair turned her stomach. She was moved to sentimental pity by the pathetic tale of the two little princes reputedly done to death within its walls, but said that anyone could see that it was just the sort of place where you could expect that kind of thing to happen. Why hadn't their Mama had the good sense to keep them safe at home with her? She, Hetty, was thankful that she lived in more law-abiding times, but had a strong presentiment that if they didn't go home soon it would be *her* bones that would be discovered in a secret grave, though *not*, she trusted, under a stairway with people tramping over her all the time.

Alethea laughed and gave it up, but she could not help wishing that Papa had been with her. He had the happy knack of bringing the past to life, of making the long dead protagonists seem vividly human and alive. He had promised to snatch a few days in Town before the end of the season if Mama could spare him. Perhaps they could revisit the Tower and she would be able to indulge her romantic imaginings to the full, freed from Hetty's prosaic commentary.

There was no sight-seeing expedition on the morning of the ball, of course. Alethea had been strictly instructed that she was to rest quietly in her room till noon. The evening's festivities would be long and arduous and it was important that she should look her very best. The thought of dawdling away a whole morning in such a wasteful fashion was irksome, but she guessed that she would be very much in the way among the bustle that was going on downstairs. She was smiling over Cowper's 'Diverting History of John Gilpin' which she had just come across in an old copy of the Public Advertiser when Hebe came in to ask if she might try her skill at dressing Miss Alethea's hair for the party.

"Hetty asked me herself, miss, knowing as she's no great hand with the curling tongs. Only I'd have to do it early, before I do madam's, if you didn't mind."

Althea had no objection at all, well knowing that the offer was a compliment of no mean order. "But I don't know about curling tongs," she added doubtfully. "Nothing seems to make it *hold* the curl. I'm sure Hetty has tried everything she knows. Don't you think it would be better just to dress it plain?"

"Well as to that, miss, and seeing we'll be early and still plenty of time to use the tongs if you don't like it, I've a fancy to try it in a Pompadour. Sadly old fashioned, of course, and should by rights be powdered, but I've a notion it will suit you. It's a style that 'ud go with your dress, besides giving you an inch or two of extra height."

That settled it, of course, Alethea, at five feet three and a bit, having sadly decided that she would never, now, grow into one of those tall willowy females who adorned the pages of the fashion journals.

Lunch was a very sketchy affair, taken in the breakfast parlour, since the dining room was already arranged for the evening's festivities. The afternoon seemed endless. Aunt Maria, supervising a dozen different domestic arrangements, said frankly that she preferred to do so unaided. She knew exactly what was to be done and it was easier to do it herself than to explain to an assistant, however willing. Having extracted a promise that her aunt would rest for an hour or two before dressing for the party, Alethea wandered into the library, selected one or two books almost at random, was hunted out by the servants who had come to set up card tables for such of the older gentlemen as did not care for dancing, and took refuge in her bedroom once more. After that things were a little better, for by good fortune, one of the books she had picked up was a copy of The Castle of Otranto which had been presented to Uncle Matthew's papa by its author. Alethea, who had never been permitted to read novels, spent the next hour or two in a new world, a world so enthralling, if at times alarming, that she was able to forget the inexorable approach of the evening's ordeal.

Hetty came in with a tray of food, scolded her for trying her eyes with too much reading and insisted that she eat something. "For it's little enough of that fine supper you'll be getting, what with dancing and talking to this one and the other, let alone the excitement. So you'll just take a bite now, before I dress you."

Alethea managed to swallow a few mouthfuls of food, though she could not have said what she had eaten, and submitted herself to Hetty's ministrations, her heart beating fast, hands icy, cheeks burning, so that she wondered that it did not show. Hetty maintained a soothing flow of chatter, telling of events below stairs, especially of one or two minor crises, all happily resolved, helped her into her dressing gown and began to brush out her hair. "And remember, miss, there's plenty of time for us to curl it for you if you don't fancy this Pompy Door that Hebe's so set on. Seems she saw it in a picture and said at once it was just the thing for you, with such a quantity of hair as you've got. But if you don't like it you've only to say so," she encouraged, and went to summon Hebe.

But when Hebe's work was done and Alethea was permitted to look at herself in the mirror, there was no question of curling tongs. She looked — and stared. That was not Alethea Forester! Not only did the fashion give her that added inch of height. It gave her, besides, a quaint, youthful dignity, despite the well-worn dressing gown. And it did more. The very severity of the style, with all the hair drawn up and away from the face, revealed the beautiful modelling of the bone structure, accentuated the lovely set of the proud little head on the slim throat. As though aware of it, the girl drew herself up to her full height, tilted her chin a little, and smiled at herself in the mirror.

Hebe smiled too, well pleased with her handiwork. And Alethea, catching the smile in the mirror, turned and hugged her impulsively, kissing her cheek lightly and saying, "It's all your doing! Dear, clever Hebe! Now I shall be able to hold up my head tonight, even beside my lovely cousin."

Her two attendants exchanged a glance of private satisfaction. That was precisely what they had intended. There was even a hint of malice in Hebe's eyes as she suggested, "Don't let anyone see you, miss, until you're all dressed and ready to go downstairs. Surprise them all."

Alethea, absorbed in turning her head from side to side to study the effect from all angles, nodded absently, and Hebe went off to attend to her proper duties.

Hetty set the room to rights with swift competence and said, "I'll be back in half an hour to help you into your dress. You'll lock your door, won't you, miss?"

To Alethea's surprised enquiry she said woodenly, "To keep it a surprise, like Hebe asked you to." And then, reluctantly, since loyalty to her former nurseling still lingered on, "And because if Miss Tina was to see you, she might say something to upset you. And we don't want tears tonight, now do we?"

Alethea's clear gaze met hers squarely. "You won't get them, Hetty. Not for so paltry a cause. But if it will please you, I'll lock the door." And then suddenly she giggled. "It sounds like something out of this fantastic tale I've been reading, but I'll do it. Unless I hear the cry of 'Fire!' I'll stay close hid," she promised, with mischievous solemnity.

Chapter Six

In general Aunt Maria enjoyed giving parties. She was a capable organiser, her servants were well trained and Uncle Matthew never begrudged additional expense in the cause of hospitality. Moreover the house in Berkeley Square was admirably adapted for the accommodation of all but the very largest gatherings. The ballroom, which had been built on to the back of the house by Uncle Matthew's papa, was of unusual design. Aunt Maria, while pretending to laugh at its oddity, secretly thought it both pretty and impressive, for the late Mr. Newton had been a friend and admirer of Mr. Walpole, and though the eccentricities of Strawberry Hill were a little too much for a strong streak of common sense, he, too, had indulged his fancy for the Gothic when building the ballroom. So the cavernous hearths that yawned at either end would not have been out of place in a mediaeval fortress and the long line of windows that pierced the outer wall were lancet shaped and ornamented with much delicate tracery of stonework. Since they gave on to a conservatory only a dim greenish light filtered through them, but this, thought Aunt Maria, served to enhance the romantic atmosphere. And when the great branches of candles set in the wall sconces were all lit, the effect was quite charming, she told her awed niece. Uncle Matthew, when out of humour, had been known to stigmatise the apartment as 'a damned draughty hole,' and declare that one might as well give a party in the cellars, but his wife assured Alethea that it was most conveniently designed, for there was a gallery hung at one end for the use of the musicians, while at the other a massive oaken door gave access to the dining room, which much facilitated the serving of suppers.

"In fact it leaves only one thing to be desired," she concluded wistfully. "If only it had a staircase!"

Since the ballroom was a single storey edifice on the ground floor, Alethea looked slightly startled. But Aunt Maria explained that nothing gave a hostess such confidence as to stand regally at the head of an imposing stair to receive her guests. Especially when, like Aunt Maria, the

49

hostess was short and dumpy and apt to be overlooked when the room became crowded.

Staircase or not, Aunt Maria had need of all the confidence she could summon for this particular party. At least her new gown was very becoming, she decided, as Hebe set the finishing touches to her elaborate coiffeur, and the maid had assured her that Miss Alethea looked very nice, too. She turned to her jewel case to find the ruby pendant that she meant to present to the child to mark the occasion. She hoped Tina would not be too angry when she saw it. Tina, with her colouring, should never wear rubies, but it was a costly trifle and she might well begrudge its bestowal on her cousin. Her fingers closed nervously over it as a tap on her door heralded her daughter's arrival.

But Tina, having won her way, was in her sunniest mood. She looked quite ravishing — and knew it. The sea-green gauze had always been becoming to her glowing locks and delicate skin. Tonight she had chosen to take the pearls that Papa had given her last year and wear them threaded through her curls. Mrs. Newton was horrified, for it was obvious that the pearls had been re-strung for the purpose, and what would Papa say if any had been lost or damaged in the process? But there could be no denying that the effect was delightful. The girl looked like some faery creature — a sea-nymph, perhaps — mysterious, elusive and tantalising.

When her mama timidly disclosed her intention of bestowing the pendant on Alethea, Tina said only, "I suppose I should have bought something for her, but I forgot. Do you think it would serve if I gave her the pierced ivory fan that Aunt Georgina sent me? I never liked it above half and I have several prettier ones." And Mrs. Newton was so thankful to be spared reproaches for her own generosity that she approved this notion quite heartily and Tina went off to find the despised fan.

Alethea looked up shyly when Aunt Maria came in, magnificent in peacock blue brocade and exclaiming in warm delight at her niece's transformed appearance. Hetty discreetly vanished. Having studied the bergère gown from every angle and praised the imaginative hair style, which was, she said the perfect complement to the dress, she bent forward to fasten the ruby pendant about the slim throat. "A little gift from your uncle and me," she said affectionately, "a keepsake to remind you of this important day in your life. May it bring you memories of a delightful evening." And as Alethea stammered out her delight and gratitude and carefully kissed her aunt's delicately rouged cheek, went on, "It puts the perfect finishing touch to your appearance. I do not in general approve of young girls wearing sparkling stones, but this is very simple, and the antique setting, you see, makes it so very suitable to your costume. The whole effect puts me strongly in mind of the painting on my Watteau fan."

"And will do very well for a masquerade when she is tired of wearing it to parties." Tina had come in so quietly that they had not heard her in their absorption; had missed the abrupt check, the slight narrowing of her eyes at this first sight of her cousin in festive array. Before they could recover, she was putting the fan into her cousin's hands, praising the elegant draping of the damask and the rich glow of the ruby. The unusual hair style, too, came in for commendation. "Vastly becoming," she pronounced. "I had not thought you could look so well. Mamma must be very pleased with the result of her efforts. And with your courage, too," she added thoughtfully. "I doubt if I could have summoned the confidence to wear so outmoded a fashion at *my* début."

Perhaps because of Hetty's warning, perhaps because at last she had her cousin's measure, this unkind little speech, designed to undermine the neophyte's confidence, wholly failed of its intent. "With your looks you would win admiration whatever you chose to wear," retorted Alethea. "As for your hair, it would still look perfectly lovely even if you had just been caught in a rainstorm. I only hope this careful erection of Hebe's doesn't tumble down and disgrace me utterly as soon as I start dancing, though she swears it won't. Plain people, cousin, have to study to be neat and soignée, which is a thing you've never had to bother about." Then, feeling that the exchange had gone far enough, "Shall I carry my new fan, Aunt? It goes beautifully with my dress."

"Slip the riband over your wrist," advised Aunt Maria. "You will need your hands free for dancing. We must go down. Our guests will be arriving."

In fact they heard the front door bell ringing as they went through the hall to join Uncle Matthew. Though the cards of invitation said nine o'clock, some people, he said bitterly, would be early for their own funerals. He mellowed sufficiently to smile at his niece and to tell her she looked very pretty. His daughter earned no such encomium. His gaze rested attentively upon the pearls in her hair, and it was fortunate for Tina that at this moment the first arrivals were announced.

At the end of half an hour, Mrs. Newton was able to dismiss any lingering doubts as to the success of her party. She was even brought to admit that there had been a good deal of truth in Tina's prophecy that Lord Skirlaugh would prove to be a social asset of considerable value. Again and again as she moved from group to group or returned to her post to welcome newcomers, she caught the echo of his name. Whatever her guests might think of her daughter's behaviour, they were not disposed to miss the opportunity of making his lordship's acquaintance at a comparatively intimate party. One or two of her closest friends actually asked to have him pointed out to them.

His lordship obliged these interested parties by arriving only a little after nine in company with the Graysons. If Kit had had his way they would undoubtedly have been there sooner. As it was, there was barely time for the necessary introductions before another group of guests was announced. There was a brief discussion about dancing. Alethea found herself engaged to dance with both gentlemen and to make up a set of quadrilles with them, but was called away by her aunt to meet the newcomers before she was quite sure which would be her partner. There had been no recognition in Lord Skirlaugh's eye, no awkward disclosure. Like her aunt, she, too, forgot her anxieties and gave herself up to enjoyment.

She did not know above half the guests and those she did know were all recent acquaintances. But that only made conversation so much the more interesting. She had never before attended such a party as this, but during the past year she had frequently accompanied Papa when her mother's delicate health had prevented her from fulfilling some engagement. During a winter of sober functions she had endured and outgrown the first paralysing pangs of shyness. Because she was least in importance she had usually been given the dullest of the dinner partners and quite unconsciously had begun to acquire that most useful of all the social arts — that of inducing people to talk about themselves. Tonight's guests were very different from the church dignitaries, the forthright squires with their strong prejudices and loyalties to whom she was accustomed. She found them very interesting, even exciting. It was scarcely surprising that this appreciative attitude evoked a pleasant warmth in those who encountered it; that soon Aunt Maria was rejoiced to receive several compliments on her niece's pleasant manners and charming appearance.

When the dancing began she was less at ease. She had been carefully taught and had a certain natural grace but she had danced very little in public. She was inclined to concentrate on the steps and the figures, so that conversation languished. Presently she found herself dancing the coranto with Lord Skirlaugh who, unfortunately, was no more skilled than was his partner. He did his best to accommodate his longer steps to hers, but by the time they had circled the room they were both a little breathless and Alethea, at any rate, was on the brink of laughter, for it was funny to find that the arrogant gentleman of the coach was so inept in the ballroom.

As they neared one of the Tudor style doorways that gave on to the conservatories he drew her a little aside from the dancers who now thronged the floor. "I'm afraid I'm not very good at this sort of thing," he apologised gravely. "Would you not rather take a turn in the conservatories?"

She agreed to it willingly enough, for the conservatories were delightfully lit by strings of coloured lanterns and a number of the guests were already strolling there. As they left the brilliantly lit ballroom for the dimmer illumination outside, she put up a surreptitious hand to assure herself that her hair was still firm and neat, that the lofty erection had not tilted, ridiculously, to one side.

"Still worrying about your hair, Miss Forester?" enquired her companion, a teasing note in the deep tones. "You have no need, I give you my word. A charming style, and most becoming to you. And even after my lamentable essay in the coranto still silken smooth."

"So you *did* recognise me," she said, the words almost startled out of her.

"Of course. Though perhaps I should rather say that I was expecting to see you. And to beg your pardon for not having called upon you sooner, as I promised."

She murmured something politely evasive about not making too much of a trivial matter.

He brushed this aside. "I found a considerable press of business awaiting me on my return to Town," he explained briefly, "and, indeed, am still a good deal occupied. I did, in fact, call on your aunt about ten days ago, but was informed that she was seriously indisposed. And in my preoccupation I had foolishly left my card case at home. I fear your butler thought me a very queer kind of visitor."

Alethea was aware of distinct satisfaction that he had, after all, kept his promise, for his failure to do so had sorted ill with her assessment of his character. But predominant at the moment was irrepressible amusement. All the fuss as to whether this particular gentleman should, or should not be invited to the party, and if only Tina had waited another day or two everything would have fallen smoothly into place.

"May I not share the joke?" asked his lordship.

"Joke, milord?"

"Yes. I do not have to stand on ceremony with you, do I, Miss Forester? The circumstances of our first meeting made us" — he hesitated for the word, then said — "comrades-in-arms," saw her face light with pleasure and went on confidently, "so let us not waste time in conventional exchanges about the excellence of the music, the beauty of the conservatories, or, alas! the lamentable performance of some of the dancers. Permit me instead to point out to you that you are standing immediately beneath one of these artistically disposed lanterns, and since you have not yet had time to acquire the social mask that hides all natural feeling, your face is a pretty accurate reflection of your sentiments." He smiled down at her quizzically as he marked off on his fingers, "First you were not sure that I had recognised you. Then you were quite pleased that I had, but far more pleased that I had kept my word about calling upon your aunt. And then" — he touched his third finger — "something occurred to you that amused you so much that your whole prim little face crinkled into laughter. Oh dear! I should not have said that! But so it looked. Forgive me, pray!"

She had to laugh. And what harm could it do to tell him? Just a little. And without giving herself further time for reflection she said, "It is only that my aunt and my cousin have been quite at outs over you. My cousin, remembering you from Marianne's party, wished you to be invited to mine, while my aunt held fast by convention, insisting that to send you an invitation when she was not personally acquainted with you would be encroaching. Yet if they had only known of our meeting — of your intention to pay your respects in form" — she bubbled into laughter again.

"Did they not know of our meeting, then?"

The laughter snapped off. "Why yes! In one sense. But it so chanced that your *name* was not actually mentioned." And then, shamefaced, but determined to make a clean breast of it, "And I did not tell about changing my gown in your coach. Somehow" — she pressed her fingers to burning cheeks — "it seemed so peculiar. Not the action itself, but the telling of it." The serious brown eyes implored him.

He nodded gravely. "Yes, indeed. A most awkward situation to describe to anyone. And your gov — er — chaperone? Miss Heatherfield was it? She did not mention it either?"

"Miss Hetherstone. No. As I recall, we were interrupted. And she went home to the Wells next day, so there was no opportunity for explanations."

There was a deep tuck in the unscarred cheek but his voice betrayed no hint of amusement as he said, "Then it seems to me we had best forget that bit of the story. It would be foolish to pretend that we had never met before, but so far as your relatives are concerned your knowledge of my identity might well begin tonight. I only hope," he added reflectively, "that you did not paint me in too unchivalrous a light."

She blushed, and stammered a little, remembering her first opinion of the gentleman who was now being so kind and helpful. "I do not quite like to deceive my aunt," she hesitated.

"You are not deceiving her. You are telling the truth — and, I daresay, helping her out of an awkward situation. If it is known that you and I were already acquainted — that I had actually — er — been of some service to you on your journey to Town?" There was a mischievous grin for that. "Would not that make all smooth?"

Before she could decide what was best, her next partner appeared hovering in the doorway.

"I must make my peace with your aunt," he told her, resigning her to the new claimant, "and I shall hope to make a better showing in the quadrilles."

Perhaps because of his height it seemed as though her glance was continually falling upon him whenever she looked about the room. She saw him dancing with Marianne and then with Tina; engaged in conversation with her uncle and another older man; and once, in earnest conversation with her aunt. On that occasion Aunt Maria turned to look at her and smiled across the room. She guessed that his lordship had taken matters into his own hands. Arrogant? Overbearing? Perhaps. She could only feel grateful to him for sparing her an embarrassing task. It had been well done, too, for a little while later Aunt Maria summoned her with a glance and said happily, "What a fortunate chance that it should have been Lord Skirlaugh who came to your assistance on your way to Town! If *only* you had been aware of his identity! I know you will not mind, my dear. I have mentioned the incident to one or two of my friends. Just casually, of course. You must see that it puts quite a different complexion on his presence here." And Alethea need only smile and nod and turn again to her impatient partner.

When the sets for the quadrilles were formed she found that she had Kit Grayson to partner her. Her cousin was dancing for the second time with Lord Skirlaugh and the set was made up by Marianne, a brother and sister called Borrodaile and a very young gentleman, little more than a schoolboy, whose name escaped her. Kit was apt to be gazing at Tina when he should have been attending to the figure and frequently had to be recalled to his place, but fortunately everyone took it in good part and except for losing him completely in the grande ronde they brushed through tolerably well, and moved in a laughing group towards the supper room.

They were all warm and thirsty after their exertions. Alethea, unaccustomed to wine, accepted the cool bubbling drink that Kit brought her, drank it thirstily, and permitted him to refill the glass. Having thus fulfilled his social obligations he turned the rest of his attention to her cousin, but fortunately for Alethea her other neighbour was young Martin Borrodaile and they were soon getting on famously. Martin was an officer in the Navy and presently it emerged that he had been engaged in the recent battle of the Saintes. The shy youngster — he was a cornet of Hussars and everyone called him Gilbert, though Alethea still did not know whether that was his first name or his surname — awoke to sudden eloquence and plied him with eager questions. Marianne and Alethea joined in. Very soon, with the aid of a selection of cutlery and one or two neglected dishes, he was demonstrating just how Rodney's 'Formidable' had broken through the French line so that de Grasse's ships had been overwhelmed. Alethea sipped her wine and nibbled an apricot tart and felt very happy.

Young Gilbert volunteered the information that he had good cause to be grateful to Lord Rodney since it was thanks to his lordship that supplies had been got through to Gibraltar when the garrison was in desperate case. Everyone looked very much surprised since he seemed far too young to have been concerned with that beleaguered fortress, whereupon he blushed hotly and explained that it was his brother who had actually been one of the defending garrison. "But m' parents would never have let me join if Henry hadn't come off safe." Martin Borrodaile promptly exclaimed at coincidence. *His* brother, too, a Marine officer, had been one of Gibraltar's defenders.

Tina, who soon grew bored with any conversation that did not centre upon herself, broke in upon the enthusiasts at this point to say how much she wished that she had been born a boy so that she, too, might have gone for a soldier and had adventures. The two young gentlemen listened respectfully, Kit protested vehemently and Lord Skirlaugh made no comment at all. Feeling that the gambit had not met with the response that it deserved, Tina appealed prettily to the young ladies to support her view. Marianne and young Jennifer Borrodaile looked dubious, but such was the force of Tina's personality that they hesitated to differ, and Jennifer, who had conceived a girlish admiration for the dashing Miss Newton, went so far as to announce that if *she* had been born a boy she would have run away to sea.

"And the first time you saw a rat in the bread locker you'd have screamed the place down," grunted her brother with tolerant amusement, "let alone being sea sick before your unfortunate vessel had so much as weighed anchor."

"And what does Miss Forester say?" enquired Lord Skirlaugh, taking pity on Jennifer's abashed face.

Miss Forester, following her aunt's advice about never putting herself forward, had so far maintained a discreet silence. But in the face of direct challenge — and fortified by two glasses of Mr. Newton's best champagne — she put up her chin and eyed his lordship defiantly. "I much prefer being a girl," she told him coolly. "I like wearing pretty clothes and going to parties and having gentlemen open doors for me and rise when I enter a room. And as for adventures, I should dislike them extremely." Her mind returned for a moment to the novel she had read that afternoon. "They sound horribly uncomfortable. While as for being shut up in a fortress like Gibraltar" — she turned to the young Hussar — "short of food and ammunition, a powerful enemy bombarding the place and little hope of rescue or relief, I should be absolutely terrified and certainly quite useless."

Everyone laughed, except Tina, who felt that this prosaic view had made her look slightly ridiculous. But worse was to come.

"Yet when a real adventure came your way," said Lord Skirlaugh quietly, "you were neither terrified nor useless, were you, Miss Forester? As I remember it, you dealt very competently."

Naturally everyone — save Tina — was all agog, plying him with questions, demanding to be told the whole story. Alethea, scarlet-cheeked, assured them that it was all a hum — merely a matter of tending an injured colt. Lord Skirlaugh, eyes dancing with a mischief they had not reflected in years, made matters worse by solemnly assuring them that his lips were sealed. She could only be thankful when the young soldier, abandoning what he took to be a private joke, began to talk to her about the siege of Gibraltar and to tell her about the red-hot shot, which, he had been told, the garrison had used with considerable success. She was thankful enough to give him her whole attention, and at the end of a brisk exchange he told her, with schoolboy bluntness, that for one who claimed to like only fal-lals and fripperies and not to care for adventure; she was singularly well-informed on military matters. For a girl, he qualified, with a candour he might have used to a sister.

"Oh — my cousin dotes on fusty old historical things," intervened Tina with tinkling sweetness. "I believe she had rather be poking about the dungeons in the Tower than attending an Assembly. Even Papa is quite exhausted by her zest for knowledge, and Mama and I tell her that she is quite shockingly 'blue'. I daresay it comes of having a parson for a father and being brought up so simply in the country, but she will have to make a push to mend her ways or she will stand in danger of becoming a dead bore."

There was a horrid little silence. The tender-hearted Marianne winced. The younger members of the party looked anywhere but at Alethea, until the boy who had talked of Gibraltar said indignantly, stuttering in his fervour, "B-but I *wasn't* b-bored! N-never b-been so well pleased at a party before. Talk that a fellow can understand and enjoy. What's wrong with that?"

Tina had been at once aware that she had blundered. To see another girl the focus of attention — and that girl her mousy country cousin — had been more than she could endure. She had permitted jealousy to outrun discretion — revealed the claws that lay hid beneath the charming surface. And that in front of the one man whom she had most wished to impress with her sweetness and serenity. But something could still be salvaged. This raw stammering cub could be ignored. She took her cue from the sound of violins being tuned and rose, smiling brilliantly at Kit.

"This is our dance, is it not? We must not waste it." And as her docile swain rose and offered his arm, she paused and tapped Alethea's cheek with a slender finger. "Don't look so downcast, cousin. Remember that Mama expressly charged me to see that you comported yourself modestly in society."

But not at her coming-out party. And not in so public a fashion, thought Damon grimly. Even if the set-down had been justified, which it certainly was not. The bitch! And then, remembering certain faithful companions of his boyhood and one ancient deerhound who still supervised his comings and goings at Byram, hastily withdrew the epithet. It was too good for that spiteful creature.

He looked covertly and with dawning respect at Miss Forester's composed little face. Only the tight set of the childish lips betrayed her. Not *too* sympathetic, now, or her control might snap, and she would never forgive him.

"It seems that we share another interest, Miss Forester, apart from horse-flesh," he said pleasantly. "I, too, have an affection for historic buildings. And even, perhaps more, for such places as Byram, which have never reached the pages of the history books but are still steeped in ancient wisdom and mystery. In fact I have sometimes fancied that a building becomes imbued with some essence of the people who have lived and loved and suffered in it. Tell me, have you ever visited Hampton Court Palace?"

Chapter Seven

There had been no further opportunity for conversation but Damon had no intention of letting matters rest there. Having offered Miss Forester his support, he meant to make good his word. Not that the little thing was unable to stand up for herself, he reflected, with a gleam of humour. She had been taken by surprise — as, indeed, had they all. Now that she was warned he rather suspected that she would give a good account of herself, though she would be sorely handicapped by her position as a guest in her cousin's home.

In one particular, however, he still misread the situation. He assumed, as he had done from the start, that Alethea was a poor relation being sponsored into society by her wealthy aunt. Tina's remarks had seemed to confirm this belief, even though there had been nothing poverty pinched about the girl's appearance last night, he reflected, as he trod up the steps of the Newton town house and set the bell pealing.

He had timed his arrival with care. As he had expected, he was told that Mrs. Newton was not at home. Probably still fast asleep, he translated, and who should blame her? An enquiry for Miss Forester produced a distinct stiffening in the butler's benevolent air. A real gentleman ought to know that the young lady couldn't receive him, not without her aunt was there.

"As to that, I couldn't say, m'lord," he said woodenly. "I will cause enquiry to be made if you wish it."

"No, don't do that," returned his lordship affably. "But I'd be grateful if you'd have a message carried to her, if she's awake. Ask her if she will drive out with me in the Park in — let us say — an hour's time. But on no account to disturb her if she's still sleeping."

That was more the style, approved Ponting, ushering this very early morning visitor into the small saloon and going off in search of Miss Forester's maid. He quite regretted the cold reception he had accorded his lordship at their first encounter. Not often he missed his guess, but with the household in such a turmoil and the gentleman with that shocking ugly scar on him, and then no visiting card — well — anyone could make a mistake. And he didn't seem to bear no malice. Spoke pleasant enough, and him a duke's son. *And* with some sense in his cockloft, since it was Miss Forester he was asking for and not Miss Newton.

He returned very shortly to inform the visitor that Miss Forester was happy to accept of his invitation. She would be ready punctually at eleven. He, in his turn, was very happy to accept of the coin that slid so easily into his palm. The realisation that it was a half guinea and not the shilling that he had first thought, caused him to hand the caller his hat and gloves with a benignity that bordered on the paternal. His lordship, well pleased with the success of his timing, sprang up into the curricle and told Judd that they would drive about the streets for half an hour or so to take the edge off a pair that was by far too fresh for the comfort of a female passenger. Judd received this information with the impassivity of the well-trained servant, and thought his own thoughts.

Coming on nicely, they ran. So it's driving a lady in the Park, now, is it? And her to sit on his left where she can't but see the bad side of his face. Well heaven send it's the nice little piece from Tunbridge Wells and not that flytesome red-head. A rare handful *she* was, by all accounts. A beauty, if you liked the fiery sort, though for his part he fancied something more cuddlesome, and no kindness in her, if those that served her were to be believed.

When the bays drew up once more in Berkeley Square he was gratified to discover that his master's tastes endorsed his own, even though he had some difficulty in identifying the elegant young lady who came swiftly down the steps to the waiting curricle with the girl whom he remembered from that month-old roadside adventure. He thought that she remembered him, though, for she smiled at him pleasantly when his master dismissed him, saying that he might have the rest of the day to himself.

Alethea settled herself comfortably in her lofty seat, declined the offer of a rug, and, for sheer joy of driving out on so fine a morning, smiled up at her escort. "I have never ridden in a sporting carriage before," she told him. "At home I drive the gig when Papa is not using it, and in Town I have driven out with Aunt Maria in the landaulet. But this is much more exciting, as well as extremely comfortable."

She did not tell him that she had accepted his invitation with considerable misgiving for fear of what Tina would make of it. Hetty, misunderstanding her hesitation, had assured her that it was perfectly proper to drive out alone with a gentleman — "though only in an open carriage, mind," and Alethea, who dearly longed to go, had allowed herself to be persuaded. Surely so innocent an excursion could not give cause for complaint. Besides, as Hetty pointed out, it would be downright wasteful to miss such a chance of displaying the new carriage dress which had only been delivered yesterday.

Damon had noticed the dress immediately, partly because it was brown, yet presented so marked a contrast to that despised garment that Hetty had bundled away to be given to some deserving underling. It was made in heavy corded silk, cut in imitation of a man's coat and waistcoat, with overlapping revers and wide spreading skirts. This severe simplicity was relieved at the throat by a cascade of crisp frills in a shade between pink and orange that masqueraded as a neckcloth, and by the luxuriant trimming of ostrich feathers, dyed to cream and flame and bronze, that weighted the brim of the high-crowned hat that went with it. Aunt Maria was doing the thing in style, decided Damon. She, at any rate, seemed to have her niece's welfare at heart and was sparing no expense to give the girl a chance.

Conversation was limited to surface courtesies until the Park was reached. The streets were crowded, and even so capable a whip as Lord Skirlaugh had to bestow most of his attention on his horses. Alethea was well content to gaze about her with bright-eyed interest. The infinite variety of the London scene was still new to her. Presently she said shyly, "Should we not have turned to the right at that corner? I do not know London very well yet, but" —

He smiled, but shook his head. "Yes, if we had wished to go to *Hyde* Park. I had thought rather of taking you to the Green Park. It is much quieter — a great favourite with nursemaids and children — and not near so fashionable. I am afraid that delightful rig you are wearing will be sadly wasted. But at least we shall not be compelled to stop every two or three minutes to acknowledge the greetings of half the people who were at your party last night, and since I wished for a little uninterrupted conversation with you the Green Park held more appeal. I think you will like it — and since there is no great distance between the two, we may drive back by way of Hyde Park if you so wish."

She had blushed a little at the implied compliment in the remark about her dress. She might have told him that it was not wasted, since he, at least, had remarked it approvingly, but chose instead to speak of her surroundings, saying, "It is very pretty here — and more like true country than Hyde Park, though I enjoyed watching all the people there when my aunt took me driving, and the beautiful horses. But I must not be from home too long this morning. Aunt Maria was quite exhausted by last night's festivities and she may need me. What was it that you wished to say?"

Damon's lips twitched. It was four years since he had mingled freely in society, but he still remembered with distaste the arch advances, the coy withdrawals that passed for conversation with most of the débutantes. 'La, sir! What *can* you mean?' they would say, or 'Oh fie! You shock me, sir. Indeed you must not speak so bold.' And that if you but thanked them with common courtesy for the pleasure of a dance. It was a refreshing change to meet a damsel who believed in direct dealing and asked him in the most natural fashion what it was he wanted with her.

He did not, however, feel that he could quite match her frankness. He had not even fully weighed his motives in seeking her society, save that he had been disgusted by her cousin's ill-bred behaviour in reading her a public lecture and that his sympathies had been enlisted by the gallant manner in which she had met the attack. He could scarcely put all that into words. He said temperately, "Why nothing of any vast importance, Miss Forester. I had not understood, you see, that your time was not your own, and I thought you might be interested to hear the end of our adventure. I could scarcely embark upon the tale last night. Your cousin would have thought me a dead bore! And then I was hopeful of securing your promise to visit Hampton Court with me if we could arrange a time when you have no other engagements." Which ought to show her where *my* sympathies lie, he thought with satisfaction.

She surprised him again. There was quite a noticeable silence while she considered his remarks. He could not know that behind the sober little face a whole tangle of emotions fought for expression. Family loyalty won. She said seriously, "I think you are under some misapprehension, milord. My time *is* my own. Aunt Maria would be the last person to deny me any rational enjoyment. But she has been so good to me that naturally I would not wish to neglect any attention that might contribute to her comfort." She hesitated, then went on bravely, "And I think you did not quite like it when my cousin reproved me last night. But my aunt *had* asked her to show me how I should go on. So while I confess that I did not *enjoy* the rebuke, I have to acknowledge its justice."

"So do not I," said Damon shortly. "Your cousin, my girl, spoke out of sheer jealously, because for one moment you occupied the centre of the stage that she has always been accustomed to claim by virtue of her beauty."

Loyalty and honesty warred within her. "Perhaps," she temporised. "But she *is* so very lovely that she has grown accustomed to being the centre of attention."

"Oh yes, indeed! A diamond of the first water," he returned lightly. "And now may we forget her? I am longing to tell you the tale of my dealings with Master Ralph's father. You will be delighted to hear that the bay colt is well on the way to recovery and that 'Squoire' was hopeful that, though scarred, he had many years of useful life ahead of him."

"Oh! How perfectly splendid!" she exclaimed in unfeigned delight.

He pulled out a pocket book and took a letter from it, handing it to her to read as the horses dropped to a collected walk. There were two pages in a sprawling forceful hand, the first devoted to details of the treatment that was being used to restore the colt to full vigour and to minimise the scarring, with a request for any advice that might be helpful in such a case. There followed thanks for the care that had been bestowed on the animal and quite an animated account of the shifts to which the writer had been put in his efforts to trace his benefactor, an end which had been achieved at last by the happy accident of Judd's having let fall his master's name in the post boy's hearing.

"I wrote to him at once," explained Damon as she handed the letter back, "giving him such hints as I could that might prove useful, though I daresay he is far more experienced than I in such matters, and enquiring for his son. The answer came yesterday."

The letter was shorter this time, and again most of it dealt with the colt's continued improvement. There was a hearty offer of hospitality should his lordship chance to be in the vicinity, so that he might see for himself how well the gash had healed, and a brief postscript.

"My son is well enough. Better than he deserves. I gave him a rare trimming for his folly and forbade him to drive my horses until he has mended his ways. So he is still in the sullens."

Alethea smiled. "One almost feels sorry for Master Ralph. His father seems far more concerned for the horse. And it was not his fault that the man on the stage gave him spirits and made him so horridly drunk. But Papa says it is most important for a young man to learn how much he can safely drink and still behave like a gentleman, so perhaps it is as well that

Master Ralph should learn that lesson now. I expect he was very sorry when he saw what had happened to the poor horse."

"If not then, I daresay he was heartily penitent by the time his father was done with him," retorted Damon. "I think we may safely leave his education in his father's hands and consider our own interests for a while. What do you say to my notion of visiting Hampton Court Palace? It is old, it is very beautiful, and it has a history as romantic and enthralling as any I know. And it so happens that a cousin of my mother's lives there. Most of the rooms were made into private residences, you know, after the King himself declined to live there — so I am pretty well acquainted with the place. It would give me great pleasure to show it to someone who has a fondness for such things."

Alethea could think of nothing that she would enjoy more, but unfortunately that was not the only consideration. "It sounds perfectly delightful," she said, in a rather stiff little voice, "but I would have to ask Aunt Maria's permission before accepting your very kind invitation."

He supposed that in her inexperience she was doubtful about the propriety of undertaking such a prolonged expedition under male escort. He said casually, "I thought we might wait for a really sunny day and use my mother's landau. It's a trifle antiquated, but extremely comfortable for all that. Marianne has been teasing me ever since I came back to take her to visit Aunt Emily — we have always called her 'aunt' because she is a good deal older than Mama. You would not object to including my cousin in the party? She had no great interest in history, but she would be happy to bear Aunt Emily company and exchange family news while we indulge our taste for antiquity."

When his companion only smiled politely and said that that sounded very pleasant, he did not press her further, and once the question of acceptance had been safely left in abeyance, her manner became more natural. She wondered why His Majesty should have taken a dislike to the Palace. Was it true that it was haunted? Could *that* be the reason? And could *anyone* live there?

He smiled a little at her eager curiosity, which left him in small doubt that the proposed expedition was very much to her taste, and explained that his aunt had come by her tenancy because her mother had been one of Queen Caroline's ladies. Growing old, and being of an independent nature, she had disliked the idea of being a pensioner on her son-in-law's bounty — and His Majesty had been graciously pleased to grant her the use of an apartment at Hampton Court for the term of her life. As for the Palace being haunted — well — there were usually such stories told of any ancient building that had harboured tragedy and despair. The ghost of Queen Katherine Howard was reputed to haunt a certain gallery leading to the Chapel Royal. She was said to have run along it in an attempt to reach the king with a plea for mercy. But all old buildings creaked and groaned and a lively imagination could read a good deal into the strange noises that they produced. Certainly his present majesty's aversion to the place had nothing to do with ghosts. If report spoke truly, it stemmed from an occasion when his grandpapa, King George the Second, had lost his temper with him and boxed his ears — in public, too, an insult which had never been forgotten.

Only when Damon broke off to enquire whether she would like to drive home by way of Hyde Park did Alethea realise how swiftly time had fled. She exclaimed in dismay when he told her that it was long past noon, and said that she must go home at once.

Obediently he turned the curricle and urged the bays to greater effort, suggesting pleasantly that perhaps she would drive out with him again and adding, as they turned into Berkeley Square once more, "And you will let me know which day would be convenient for our visit to Hampton Court, so that I can make arrangements with Marianne."

"If Aunt Maria says I may go," she agreed, gathering her skirts with one hand in readiness to descend from the curricle.

He bowed, and she reached up her hand in farewell, thanking him formally for a delightful morning and curtseying slightly before she turned to run up the steps. He watched the door close behind her before setting the bays in motion again. A pleasant little creature, refreshingly lacking in artifice, honest and loyal, he thought approvingly, before dismissing her from his thoughts and turning with a groan to contemplation of the tasks that would have to be accomplished in payment for his morning's holiday.

Chapter Eight

Both ladies had secret misgivings. But Alethea dearly wished to accept his lordship's invitation and Aunt Maria was equally anxious to convince herself that Tina's interest in that gentleman had waned. She had not so much as mentioned his name since Alethea's party. Doubtless his facial scars had been too much for her. Besides, the projected outing would not be at all to *her* taste. Had she not regularly evaded Kit Grayson's eager pleas that she should accompany his sister and himself on one of their periodic visits to Lady Emily? Mrs. Newton refused to believe that the substitution of Lord Skirlaugh for Kit might change her daughter's attitude. So Alethea was directed to write a pretty note to his lordship, informing him of her aunt's approval, so that his arrangements could be set forward.

Alethea had been carefully taught to set small value on outward show, but she could not quite suppress her regret that Mama and Susan could not see her stepping into the Duchess of Byram's landau. Lord Skirlaugh might deprecate its shabbiness, explaining that his mama so rarely came to Town that it had not seemed worth while to have it re-furbished, but the only sign of shabbiness that Alethea could see was a slight fading of the lining from vivid gold to a soft and pleasing amber. She stole a respectful glance at the crest which adorned the door that his lordship himself opened for her, and decided that Papa would certainly rebuke her for so easily succumbing to the glamour of worldly trappings. But she had never ridden in so elegant a vehicle before, and she did not propose to allow moral reflections to spoil her pleasure.

That pleasure was increased when, as soon as the paved streets were left behind, his lordship enquired if the ladies would like the top lowered so that they might see better. Since it was a sunny morning with a promise of greater heat to come, they agreed with enthusiasm. And even Papa, thought Alethea, must have approved of the way in which his lordship sprang down and went to lend a hand with the job. Nothing consequential about *that* — and the poor man could not help his birth. She was quite sorry to think how sadly she had misjudged him at their first meeting, but there — if a man

67

was so foolishly sensitive about his appearance, he must expect to be misunderstood from time to time.

His lordship, settling back into his seat surveyed his two guests with approval and a happy sense of holiday, thankful that the long drawn out conferences with his father's agent and lawyer were done at last. Marianne had always been his favourite cousin. She had a gentleness that seemed to him truly feminine, and a quiet sense of humour that peeped out when she was not overshadowed by more strident companions. As for little Miss Forester, she looked surprisingly pretty this morning. Excitement and fresh air had brought colour to her cheeks, and though she had little to say it was obvious that she was hugely enjoying herself. Even as he watched, she sketched the faintest possible acknowledgement to a hawthorn tree that, in its array of blossom, might pass for a lady in court dress. There was a gracious gesture of one slim hand for a young horse that came trotting up to the hedge to watch their passing. Playacting, mused Damon, biting back a smile. And why not? She was little more than a child. Probably saw herself as a princess, or as Cinderella, riding to a ball. He relaxed in peaceful enjoyment of a perfect May morning, grateful that his guests did not seem to desire an uninterrupted flow of animated conversation, but rousing himself occasionally to point out such features as might be of interest to Miss Forester, since to Marianne they were already perfectly familiar.

They had left Town betimes, since they were to partake of an early luncheon with their hostess before setting out on their exploration of the ancient palace. It was not until they had passed Bushey Park, failing, to Alethea's disappointment, to catch a glimpse of the famous tame deer, but much impressed by the glory of the chestnut blossom, that it occurred to his lordship that it might be as well to warn Miss Forester of some of his aunt's eccentricities.

"Don't be surprised at anything she may say," he advised. "She is forthright to a degree, and will say exactly what comes into her head if she so chooses. Marianne will bear me out that the best way is to stand up to her. She cannot abide what she calls 'mealy-mouthed simpering'."

Alethea was somewhat alarmed by this daunting description, but comforted herself with the thought that Lady Emily was unlikely to pay much attention to her insignificant self. And at first sight her hostess's appearance was reassuring. She was slight and small, no taller than Alethea, though she held herself very erect, and her white hair was piled high on her head in an elaborate coiffeur that had been fashionable in her hey-day and was, in fact, very becoming. Closer inspection revealed a pair of bright dark eyes, a dominant nose and a wide, thin-lipped mouth, all of which conveyed a strong suggestion that this was no sweet old lady who could be written off as a nonentity. However she greeted her visitors with due civility and acknowledged Damon's presentation of Alethea with friendly welcome. If the bright eyes were agleam with curiosity they held no malice, and though she scolded Damon for extravagance in bringing her flowers when the Palace gardens were ablaze with them she was plainly pleased by the attention.

During luncheon they touched lightly on a number of topics, ranging from the scandalous mismanagement of the late war against what Lady Emily still described as 'our American colonies', to the encroaching ways of a number of shabby-genteel persons who had been permitted to take up residence at the Palace. Her ladyship could not imagine what the Lord Chamberlain was thinking of. Since Damon wickedly encouraged her to enlarge on this theme with fluent acerbity, Alethea very soon understood why it was not desirable that her ladyship should reside with her married daughter. So forceful a personality would not take kindly to the management of others, however well-intentioned.

It was at this point that she realised that Lady Emily had turned the whole of that penetrating intelligence upon herself. Casually, skilfully, she was being subjected to a searching inquisition as to her birth, breeding and social standing. Half annoyed, half amused, she answered her ladyship's questions with calm composure. She had nothing to hide and nothing to fear, so she was even able to admire the artistry of the approach. Her ladyship nodded her satisfaction.

"H'm! Good blood — and it shows. You're nothing out of the way to look at, but there's quality in you. Good manners, too. You didn't like my questioning you so close, but you suffered an old woman's impertinence and answered me fairly and with courtesy." And then — could it be apologetically? — "I'm very much out of the world these days. If I wish to know anything I have to find it out for myself. But you'll do, my gel. Believe me, you'll do."

Damon, who had been listening to this exchange with an uneasy notion that something unusual was afoot but nothing that a fellow could put a finger on, heard Alethea say gently, "You do me too much honour, ma'am. It is only thanks to the combined efforts of my parents and my Aunt Maria that I have the least idea how to comport myself in society. I go in constant dread of doing the wrong thing. It seems it is all too easy to be stigmatised as 'fast' or, perhaps worse still, 'a dead bore'. But I am grateful for your ladyship's kindly encouragement and I shall study to improve."

Her ladyship chuckled. "Think you've put me in my place, don't you, miss? And very neatly and politely, too. I don't blame you. I like a gel with spirit." She turned her attention abruptly to her young relatives. "So you've made up your mind to it at last, have you? Looking about you for a wife — or so your Mama informed me in her latest letter. High time, too. Twenty-eight, isn't it? And doubtless set in your selfish ways like the rest of your sex. You'll find yourself a crusty old bachelor eccentric if you don't make haste. And then what's to become of Byram? Your family have never figured prominently in the history books — which speaks well for their judgement and good sense — but they have always cherished and served their land. Failing heirs of your body, it would fall to your Cousin Barnard — and we all know what he is! A man-of-the-town if ever I saw one. What he didn't spend on his light-skirts would be squandered at the gaming tables. It wouldn't take him long either," she added reflectively, "since he never had any luck to offset his stupidity. And Byram's coffers are not deep enough to stand that sort of nonsense. You must look about you for a well-born heiress. Not too young, but a sensible wench who would know her duty. Such a one would suit you to a nicety, since you are, thanks be, past the age of falling in love."

Damon had endured this extremely personal diatribe with commendable good humour, but when Lady Emily added, on a suddenly sharpened note, "Not thinking of offering for your cousin, I hope. That would never do. As like as not to breed a moon-calf," his mouth tightened ominously. Seeing him on the brink of impetuous and probably extremely blunt speech, Marianne swiftly intervened.

"Set your mind at rest, aunt," she said, sweetly mischievous, "for I wouldn't have him. The kindest of cousins, but *not*, do you think, a comfortable husband? His notions are so very fusty! Why, when Mama was telling him how it was the custom in her younger days for ladies to receive especially favoured gentlemen in their dressing rooms to advise them on the final stages of their toilets, he said he thought it was most improper. Poor Mama was *quite* taken aback. And not all her assurances could convince him that such a practice was perfectly commonplace. All he would say was that no wife of his would ever be permitted so to flout his authority. So when you say that he would not do for me, you are very right."

Since Marianne was the most gentle and biddable girl and would undoubtedly make a pattern wife, Aunt Emily was not deceived by this gallant attempt to deflect her attack, but she had recognised Damon's annoyance and was very ready to accept the offered loophole. She made a fighting withdrawal, pointing out tartly that it was small wonder that Marianne was still unwed in her fourth season, so pert as she was growing, but put out a hand to draw the girl down to sit beside her on the couch and added in gentler tones, "Now you shall tell me all the news of your mother and Kit while Skirlaugh takes Miss Forester to see the sights. You'll probably have to pay for the privilege," she warned that gentleman. "There's no decent respect these days. *My* guests, having to pay a fee to view the State Apartments! They don't dare extort it if *I'm* with 'em," she went on with relish, "but you can't expect me to trail about with you at my time of life just to save your pocket. Be off with you, now, and don't walk this poor girl off her feet."

Damon said mildly that he thought he might manage to defray any necessary expenditure without actually having to sell out of the funds, and that he would take every care for Miss Forester's comfort. He then took Alethea's hand and made his escape swiftly before his aunt could do more than snort and damn his impudence. Outside the door of the apartment he paused, loosed his companion's fingers, and looked at her beneath quizzically lifted brows.

"You didn't mind, I hope? She's in good form, the old tartar. Pray what was she about to question you so close about your parents? Does she imagine that the families might be connected? They are not, are they?"

Alethea laughed. "Not to my knowledge. She was merely assuring herself that I am a fit and proper person to be a friend for Marianne."

He stiffened visibly, brows drawing together in outrage. "Then I make you my apologies. I deeply regret that you should have been subjected to such overbearing insolence while you were my guest."

She stared up at him, divided between amazement and amusement. He was not even aware, she thought, that his own arrogance was fully as great as his aunt's. "Oh, do, pray, come down out of the boughs," she said good-humouredly, much as she might have spoken to young Susan. "Your aunt did no more than any of society's leaders would do if she was not informed of a newcomer's background. She did it beautifully, and far more kindly than most. At least she did not enquire into the extent of my expectations! You make too much of it. Believe me, after six weeks in Town I have all the answers as pat as my Catechism. It is quite amusing to see how often it is brother Charles who takes the trick. He did so again, today, with your aunt."

"I did not know until today that you *had* a brother," said Damon, his expression still far from amused.

"Did you not? Well, he is a good deal older than Susan and me, and he is usually abroad. But for all that he is my greatest social asset. A clergyman for a father is merely respectable, but a brother in the diplomatic service commands much more attention. Which gives food for some interesting speculation as to the relative importance of this world and the next," she suggested demurely, but with a sideways tilt to her head and a quivering dimple that invited him to share the joke.

He had to smile. "It seems that Aunt Emily is not the only one with an edge to her tongue," he told her, and his smile deepened as he recalled his instinctive belief that this girl would give a good account of herself in a battle of words and wits. The bleak look vanished, his anger dispelled by her sunny good humour, and he was just about to claim her sympathy for the raking down that he himself had got from Aunt Emily when she stopped short and put out a hand to clutch his sleeve on a long-drawn, "Oh!" of wonderment.

They had come, in the course of their argument, to the head of the King's Staircase. Damon smiled indulgently. She was but a child, after all, to be so carried away by the lavish display of the painted walls and ceiling. For his part, he did not know which he disliked more — the exuberance or the flat conventionality — but that was no reason to spoil the child's pleasure in them. He held his tongue. And then saw the down-bent head and realised that she was not even looking at the paintings.

It was the delicate wrought-iron balustrade that had caught her attention. With one tentative finger she was lovingly smoothing the curve of a leaf. Her voice sank to a whisper as she said, "So perfect! Just think of the infinite patient toil that must have gone to its making."

Once again she had surprised him. When she bestowed only polite praise on the concourse of classic gods and goddesses, his interest deepened. Her tastes were fresh and her own. At the end of an hour's strolling progress she had lingered long over the mantel carvings in the King's State Apartments, dismissed the classical paintings with a cool, "I daresay they are very pretty but I prefer the portraits," and seemed, in general, more interested in the people who had lived in the rooms than in the faded magnificence that was displayed for the admiration of visitors. "It's not a happy palace, is it?" she said once, thoughtfully. "Those poor queens of Henry's! Well — perhaps Queen Jane was happy enough, though she didn't live to enjoy her baby, poor thing."

And when at last they emerged to stroll in the sunshine, she heaved a big sigh and said, "It's all very beautiful and romantic, but I think I like the gardens best. And I'm glad I'm just an ordinary girl living in modern times. This place has seen too much of tragedy and suffering. It's oppressive — almost as if King Henry brought a curse on it when he stole it from his friend, for it seems as though no one since his day has known lasting happiness here."

"My dear girl! You mustn't talk about kings stealing things in these royal precincts," protested Damon, laughing. "It's practically treason! King Henry would have had off your head in an instant. His Majesty was graciously pleased to accept the place as a *gift*. Come! Stop brooding over past sorrows or I shall regret bringing you. Let us see if you can find your way to the centre of King William's maze. *That* will give your thoughts a more cheerful direction."

His prescription had precisely the desired effect. It was a laughing girl who finally emerged from the maze, a little untidy as to hair, to find Marianne awaiting them.

"I saw your making for the Wilderness, so I guessed where you would be," she explained. "Aunt Emily dropped off to sleep, but I daresay she will have roused again by the time we get back. Did you enjoy it?"

By the time that Alethea had explained just how much, had washed her hands and smoothed her hair, Lady Emily was wide awake once more, obviously much refreshed by her nap, and insisting that they must take tea with her before setting out on the return journey. Her enquiries as to Alethea's opinion of the Palace were met by a laughing rejoinder from Damon, who assured her that her guest was both a barbarian and a traitor. She had not liked the Verrio paintings above half, and she had actually dared to suggest that King Henry had stolen the palace from Cardinal Wolsey.

"So he did," snapped Aunt Emily promptly. "As for the paintings — never liked 'em above half myself. A lot of naked gods and goddesses sitting about on clouds — and most of them no better than they ought to be. Pity they hadn't got something more useful to do."

This was much in Aunt Emily's usual vein. Damon and Marianne exchanged conspiratorial smiles, and settled back to sip their tea comfortably, Marianne thinking how cosy and pleasant Aunt Emily had made her little home.

Her attention was once again devoted to Alethea. "I do not believe in allowing young girls to devote too much time to the study of history," they heard her pronounce severely. "They would do better to attend to the domestic arts, so sadly neglected in these modern days. But one cannot live *here*" — she gestured widely — "without developing an interest in those who have gone before. Your King Henry, for instance," she glared at Alethea, who almost broke into urgent protest to deny any responsibility for King Henry, "was a thief, you say. What else did you expect? Was he not born of an usurper? His father stole a kingdom — and cunningly disposed of any who might threaten his position. The son, less devious, did but follow the sire's example, snatching whatever took his fancy, be it palace or bride."

"Dear me!" said Damon gently. "What a nest of treason! Such heat, Aunt Emily. You are frightening Miss Forester. Her eyes are like saucers."

"I'm not a bit frightened," exclaimed Alethea impatiently, "but oh! so interested. I never knew that other people cared about these long ago kings and queens as I do. Even Papa is more concerned with philosophical debate about the growth of democracy. Lady Emily makes them seem so human."

Lady Emily chuckled. "Yes, my gel. But I don't make 'em into saints and heroes. Kings and queens are just as faulty as lesser mortals, only larger than life because they have more power to achieve their ends."

"Do you not admire — venerate — any of them?" asked Alethea soberly.

The old lady sighed briefly. "Venerate? No. Oh! Some have had admirable qualities, no doubt. Courage, tenacity, prudence, foresight. Maybe they have made the best they could of a difficult job. And I've naught to say against our Geordie — as decent a man as you're like to find in a dissolute age, if a mite pig-headed at times. But I was bred in Yorkshire, where there are long memories and loyal hearts. There's many a one in the north would say with me that England's last true-born king was treacherously slain on Bosworth field."

She fell silent, brooding over wrongs three hundred years old, and the atmosphere she had created in those few brief sentences was not one to be lightly broken. Her young guests drank their tea in respectful silence until she roused herself suddenly, turning on Alethea with a pretence of scolding. "And what are you about, miss, beguiling an old lady to talk treasonably of a tragedy that's best left buried? You are young. You should be living in the present, enjoying a little delicate flirtation, learning how to handle a possible husband without letting him realise that he is being managed, not yearning over some long dead king. Moreover you'll think me an ungrateful wretch that bites the hand that shelters me." She raised her tea cup as though to drink a toast and said solemnly, "King George — God bless him."

Chapter Nine

As Judd drew the bays to a halt in front of the Berkeley Square house, Tina came strolling across the gardens on her way home. Alethea started guiltily. It so chanced that there had been no opportunity of mentioning the projected visit to her cousin, but she knew perfectly well that if opportunity *had* offered she would have done her utmost to look the other way.

Well — she had had her lovely day. For the sake of her two companions she hoped it would not end in an unpleasant scene. For her own part, it was worth it even if it did.

But Tina behaved beautifully. Forewarned by a careless remark dropped by Mama, she had been granted time to cool her temper and plan her campaign. She greeted them in the friendliest fashion, asking how they had enjoyed their day and then saying, with a pretty pretence of indignation, "Though I don't know why I'm so forgiving as to speak to you, wretches that you are! You *might* have given me the chance of going with you. I can't remember *how* many times I've expressed my desire to meet Lady Emily, so interesting as she must be with her memories of the past."

Neither could Marianne remember. Not one single occasion. But she was no practised dissembler. She faltered out some lame excuse about thinking that Tina would find it dull.

"Nothing of the kind," Tina assured her. "But I suppose I'll have to forgive you, because I simply *must* show you my new bonnet. Even Mama forgot to preach economy when she saw it. You'll spare her to me for a few minutes, won't you, milord?" turning her sweetest smile on Damon. "Or better still, will you not come in, too? I promise not to keep you long, and Mama will want to thank you for giving our little Thea such a delightful treat."

Alethea's eyes widened. She wondered how long she had been her cousin's 'little Thea'.

His lordship submitted to superior strategy but retained sufficient sense of self-preservation to bid Judd come back for him in half an hour.

Half an hour was quite enough for Tina. It took but five minutes to display the glories of the new bonnet. Then she and Marianne joined the others in the drawing room. In five *more* minutes, Damon found himself agreeing to make one of a party to ride in the Park next day. Marianne excused herself on the score of a prior engagement. She was not, in any case, very fond of riding, but was sure that Kit would be happy to take her place. Tina, hands clasped at her breast, face rapturous, vowed that she positively doted on the exercise and believed that 'Thea' would like it of all things.

Alethea admitted to having ridden a good deal in the country. But she had never ridden in Town and doubted if her riding dress would be modish enough by London standards. Mrs. Newton, exclaiming in dismay at such a careless oversight, said that a new habit must be ordered at once, but that something respectable could surely be contrived for the time being.

A trifle bored by this feminine chit-chat, Damon politely suggested that since there were a dozen or more horses idling their days away in his father's stable, he might be permitted to mount the ladies, and ventured tactful enquiries as to their tastes and their experience. Tina gaily announced that she could ride anything and had a preference for a chestnut. Did not his lordship think that they were, in general, more spirited?

Alethea, with every desire to take the shine out of her obnoxious cousin in the one accomplishment at which she knew herself to excel, said rather ruefully that, in so public a place, it might be wiser to choose a well-trained animal accustomed to carrying a lady.

At this point Marianne engaged Tina's attention with a laughing reference to one of her more dashing equestrian exploits, so that Damon was permitted a brief opportunity of probing this cautious statement. No, he learned. Alethea had no horse of her own. But Mama's cousin had a sizeable stable, breeding hacks and hunters, and she had learned her horsemanship from him. She was thought, she added with shy pride, to have something of a knack with nervous youngsters. Cousin Crowborough had expressed himself much obliged for her services in this respect. In return he would usually find her a horse when she had time to ride. No. She did not hunt. Did not care for it.

There was no time for more. Tina, finding that her sparkling account of a meet that she had once attended had failed to catch Lord Skirlaugh's attention, broke off to assure Marianne that she did not mean to be boring on for ever about horses, and that they must certainly arrange some pleasure party which did not involve riding for *her* entertainment.

Fortunately, before she could do so, Ponting came in to say that his lordship's carriage was waiting.

The exchange between Damon and Alethea had been brief, but his lordship was not deceived. He knew the reputation of the Crowborough stables. If Miss Forester had learned horse manège in *that* school, she was no novice. Recollection of the confident way in which she had handled a frightened, high-couraged animal confirmed this opinion. She should certainly have the well-schooled lady's mount that she had asked for, but the mare he had in mind for her use was rather more than that. A gentle, affectionate creature, responsive to the least touch of sympathetic hands, she yet had abundance of playful ways that made her sheer delight to a true horse lover.

Miss Newton's requirements posed more of a problem. He did not normally buy a horse because it was a pretty colour and he did not share Miss Newton's predilection for chestnuts. The only one in his stable at present was quite unsuitable — a half-broke youngster. He began to mull over a list of his friends. Presently his mouth curved in mischievous satisfaction as he realised that he had hit on the very thing. That peacocky gelding of Tom Milligan's! Tom had actually tried to sell him the brute — had gone the round of his acquaintance blathering about its perfections. And, to be fair, it *was* a handsome creature. Only it was all looks and no performance. A very appropriate mount for Miss Newton, he decided with regrettable cynicism, save that the animal had at least the merit of an amiable disposition. Tom would be only too happy to lend it — would crow delightedly at the thought that it was eating its handsome head off at some other fool's expense. Scribbling a note to him, Damon found that he was looking forward to his morning engagement, if not with pleasure, at least with a definite malicious interest.

And matters fell out much as he had anticipated. Miss Newton had heartily approved her cousin's riding dress, a well-worn and workmanlike garment in dark brown that provided an admirable foil for her own elegant array. Her satisfaction grew at the sight of the horses provided for the two of them. The chestnut, she felt sure, was the pride of the Duke's stable. To an undiscerning eye, the neat brown mare was not impressive. His lordship, listening appreciatively to her ecstasies, had some difficulty in keeping his countenance. He left Kit to put her up and turned to watch with amusement and satisfaction Miss Forester's very different approach. While lending a polite ear to Miss Newton's rhapsodies he had been aware of the quiet conference between groom and rider; had seen the girl finger the cheek-strap and decide that it would do, talking quietly to the animal all the while. Now he saw her automatically test the girth and nod to the groom, who handed over the reins and lifted her into the saddle without fuss. She sat there quietly, feeling the mare's mouth and, if the attentively flickering ears were any indication, maintaining the gentle monologue which would accustom the animal to the sound of her voice. Much pleased with the accuracy of his assessment, Damon swung himself into the saddle and the quartet set out for the Park.

It proved to be the first of many excursions in which he found himself involved by the persistent Miss Newton. At the outset he derived some entertainment from her skilful portrayal of artless innocence. She had a way of claiming his attention, his agreement to any suggested treat, with childish ingenuousness, making excellent play with long curling lashes and occasionally, in an access of fervour, clutching his sleeve with pleading fingers. It was a superlative performance — and when its artistry had palled, Lord Skirlaugh found it a confounded nuisance. It allowed him only the briefest snatched moments in which to improve his acquaintance with Alethea Forester. And his interest in that young lady was steadily growing. He found himself studying her reactions — the amused glint in her eye for Tina's higher flights, the tolerant acceptance of folly. On the rare occasions when he was permitted to talk to her he found her happily receptive of all that the London scene had to offer, but by no means overwhelmed. She enjoyed the social round, but would not be sorry to return to her quiet country existence. He judged her to have won a modest social success — perhaps more than might have been expected for a girl with neither rank nor fortune to recommend her. If she was not besieged by partners for every dance, neither was she left to sit forlorn with the dowagers.

But these conversations were brief. Inevitably, whenever some promising avenue opened before them, they would be interrupted. If it was not Tina herself who broke impatiently across their discussion, then it was one of her many puppets. For to Damon she seemed to manipulate the household in Berkeley Square as though they had no separate existence. Even his cousin Marianne danced to her piping and would only say plaintively, when he taxed her with it, that it was more comfortable to fall in with Tina's wishes than to run counter to them.

Nevertheless his knowledge of Miss Forester's character had advanced to the point at which he was considering, quite coolly and rationally, whether she would make him a suitable wife. He was not, of course, in the least in love with her. He had finished with that sort of nonsense once and for all when Elinor Coutance had jilted him. But he had definite ideas about the qualities that were desirable in a wife and it seemed to him that Miss Forester filled the bill quite admirably. She had dignity and self-control. She could converse sensibly on a number of topics not wholly feminine, and her gratitude to her aunt for giving her a season in Town inclined him to think that her disposition was gentle and affectionate. He knew from experience that she kept her head in emergency and showed practical good sense. He thought his mother would like her — and that was important. His father would certainly object to her lack of fortune. All the world knew that the Duke was not a wealthy man. His personal tastes were simple — many a well-to-do merchant would have thought his private expenditure ridiculously inadequate. But he had one insatiable passion — Byram. And Byram had a voracious appetite. The park and gardens, the farms and cottages, were famous throughout the land, and the old house was maintained and tended with unceasing care and at heavy expense. Its owner was not likely to welcome a penniless daughter-in-law, however admirable her character and disposition, though no doubt he could be brought to acceptance in time.

What would be Miss Forester's view of the proposition? She struck him as a level headed kind of girl who was unlikely to take a huff because he was not prepared to make pretty love speeches or vow undying passion. And without undue conceit, she could scarcely hope for a better match. She was not a beauty, though for his own part he liked her looks — far preferred them to her much vaunted cousin's. When she was happy and absorbed — which was most of the time — her face had an animation that gave the illusion of beauty. On the rare occasions when he had seen her cast down — disappointed, perhaps, or a trifle homesick — he had been conscious of a strong urge to take her in his arms and console her as one might a child. Yes, he decided contentedly, he was really quite fond of the girl. And if, at the thought of the comforting kisses that he would bestow upon that soft young mouth, some feeling much warmer, much fiercer than mere fondness quickened his pulses, it was sternly suppressed. He was endeavouring to estimate the advantages of a marriage of convenience from Miss Forester's point of view, he reminded himself.

From such details of her home background as she had let fall, he pictured a genteel family of limited means managing, with the assistance of the wealthy aunt to give the elder daughter a season in Town so that she might have the opportunity of forming an eligible connection before it was time to fire off the younger one. He heartily approved of such prudent planning. But there did not seem to be any promising suitors dangling after Miss Forester, so unless she had some romantic notion about falling in love she might be willing to consider his offer. There was the younger sister to be established, he remembered, and the brother in the diplomatic service was probably pretty expensive. A girl with a strong sense of duty would take all that into account.

Would it suffice to outweigh the one factor he had so far left out of his calculations? Would a young girl, gently bred and fastidious, find it possible to contemplate marriage with one so shockingly scarred? To be sure Miss Forester was one of the few people who never made him feel self-conscious about his appearance. He did not think she found him actually repugnant. But marriage was vastly different from occasional social encounters.

He shrugged, and abandoned speculation. There was only one sure way of discovering the answer to his doubts. But to give himself a fair chance, he felt he would like to make some attempt to fix his interest with the girl. Alethea. He tested the name aloud and liked the sound of it. How like the unpleasant Miss Newton to shorten it to the commonplace 'Thea'! That same Miss Newton was going to be a most damnable nuisance in any attempts he might make to better his acquaintance with her cousin. Let her but suspect what was in his mind and she would make the poor little thing's life a misery. He could not so expose the girl he hoped to persuade into marriage. A fine start that would be! He decided to enlist Marianne's support and went off at once to seek her out.

Marianne was delighted to be chosen as his confidante though disappointed at his prosaic approach to the business of marriage. Privately she thought that he was, perhaps, more attached to Miss Forester than he himself realised, since he was prepared to face his father's displeasure at the news that his choice had fallen on a penniless girl. Well — not precisely penniless, perhaps, but Marianne, who had naturally heard a good deal more about Alethea's home life than had Damon, doubted if her marriage portion would be above two thousand pounds. She commended his intention of paying some court to the lady of his choice before approaching her parents for permission to make her an offer, suggested one or two expeditions that would offer opportunities of tête-à-têtes, and pledged herself to do all in her power to ensure that these were granted him.

It proved to be surprisingly difficult. Whether from notions of proper conduct or from fear of annoying Tina, Alethea slipped skilfully away from anything approaching intimate conversation with Damon and stuck closely to Marianne. And if, by careful contrivance, Marianne managed to secure for him a few minutes alone with her, Tina was sure to break in upon them.

Tina was quite unperturbed by Damon's kindness for her dull little cousin. It was obviously pure charity. Unless, she thought amusedly, he was trying to make her jealous, in which case he should have chosen someone a good deal more attractive than Thea. What she did find irritating were his references to that incident on the Tunbridge Wells road. There could be no denying that he had been much impressed by Thea's behaviour on that occasion. Tina began to turn over in her mind various schemes by which she could present herself in a similarly favourable light.

The only success that the two conspirators achieved was a steadily growing friendship between Alethea and Marianne, which was very comfortable but not what they had set out to do. Yet it was this friendship which was eventually destined to bring about that much desired tête-à-tête. The two girls had reached the stage where confidences came easily, and as girls will, they talked often about the married state. They had been spending a wet afternoon in Marianne's room, Alethea trying on her friend's dresses and bonnets, a proceeding which reduced them both to helpless laughter, when Alethea suddenly said, "I just don't understand it. You're so pretty, so loveable. I know from Aunt Maria that you've had any number of chances. Don't you *like* men?"

Marianne hesitated briefly. She had guarded her secret so long. Only her mother knew of her unwavering loyalty to James Borrodaile. But now, at last, James was on his way home. Her heart was light, she was in the mood to talk of wedding plans and Alethea could be trusted not to chatter indiscreetly. So the whole story came tumbling out.

She had known the Borrodailes all her life — Alethea would remember meeting Jennifer and Martin at her party — but Mama had felt that she must have at least one season in Town and meet other gentlemen before committing herself irrevocably to James. She had nothing against the match — indeed she was very fond of James — but Marianne was so young. And life as the wife of a serving officer, with its long separations and its grave anxieties would be very hard. Let them wait a little while, be very sure that the attachment between them was strong enough to withstand the strains that would be put upon it. So they had waited. And the waiting had stretched for four interminable years, while Marianne had learned the truth of Mama's warning words, and learned, too, that parting and anxiety had only strengthened her love. Sometimes she would hear nothing for months. Then would come a whole bundle of letters when the blockade had been briefly broken. And now the long ordeal was almost over and they hoped to be married in the autumn.

Alethea listened wide-eyed. So much heartache and loneliness behind the pleasant façade of Marianne's smooth young face! She said slowly, "You must love him very much."

Marianne smiled a little. "Yes," she said. "I wish now that we had not allowed Mama to persuade us into waiting. If anything had happened to James" — she broke off, with a little shiver. Then said cheerfully, "But it didn't. He will be home any day and then we shall plan our wedding. I shall ask you and Jennifer to be my bride's maidens."

Alethea expressed her pleasure in the invitation but said hesitantly, "Not Tina? *She* was your friend before I was."

Marianne laughed outright. "Very definitely not Tina. Can you imagine any bride in her senses inviting comparison with Tina? You and Jennifer are quite pretty enough. Tina would steal the scene entirely. As for friendship" — she hesitated for a moment, then said slowly, "I know she is your cousin. Perhaps I should not say it. But Tina's friendship lasts just so long as she has use for you. My usefulness — and poor Kit's — is almost done. She needed us only to draw Damon into her circle."

Not even family loyalty could bring Alethea to deny the truth of this. "Is your brother very much hurt?" she asked diffidently.

Marianne shrugged. "He doesn't quite believe it yet. Nor realise what a fortunate escape he has had. If *he* had been a Duke's son —!"

"People are so different," said Alethea lamely. "Tina has beauty and wealth in plenty. So she yearns for high rank — the one thing she hasn't got."

"And won't get from Damon," retorted Marianne, in tones as near malicious as her soft voice could manage. "He doesn't even *like* her. If she but knew it, his thoughts are turned in quite another direction."

Alethea looked both intrigued and alarmed. "Heavens! I hope I'm safe home again before he announces his betrothal," she exclaimed lightly.

"Tina would be quite unbearable." and then, coaxingly, "Who is she? Do I know her?"

But Marianne refused to be drawn, vowing she had said too much already.

"Well, I hope, whoever she is, that she will make him happy, for the poor man has had more than his share of ill-fortune."

Such a splendid opportunity to put in a little special pleading on Damon's behalf was too good to be missed. "Yes, indeed," agreed Marianne with enthusiasm, and launched into a diatribe against that horrid wretch Elinor Coutance who had thrown Damon over after playing cat-and-mouse with him for months. "And Tina thought to entrap him by her beauty in just the same way," she ended scornfully. "Do you think she would have any use for him if he were just plain Mr. Hardendale? And scarred as he is? Have you not seen how she cannot endure to look at the injured side of his face but moves always to his right hand? Oh — she does it skilfully, casually, but she does it. And imagines he doesn't notice! Poor Damon! He told me once — it was in the early days when they still feared for his sight — that he would have endured even *that* loss, almost thankfully, if only the child had lived. It was dead when he brought it out, you know, the baby. Suffocated by the smoke, they said."

A glance at Alethea's face, the brown eyes misted with pity, decided her that she had said enough on this head "Marriage will give his life a new meaning," she went on briskly. "And she will be a fortunate girl who marries him, despite the scars."

"I shouldn't think she would notice them," returned Alethea. "They are not near so bad as he seems to imagine. After a little while one simply forgets them. They are part of him, but oh! such an unimportant part compared with his courage and his kindness."

That augured well for Damon's hopes, thought Marianne happily. But Alethea was not done. "For my part," she pronounced judicially, "I would rather be wary of his pride."

"Pride?" exclaimed Marianne, startled and indignant.

"Yes," returned Alethea firmly. "It is not really the scars that he resents so much as his own failure. If I were his chosen bride, *that* is what I should fear — his demand for perfection. How could any girl ever come up to such a standard?"

Chapter Ten

That was baying at the moon with a vengeance, thought Alethea, walking sedately homeward with Hetty. But a girl must have *some* kind of shield against a man who was not for her, and who, scars or no, could win her heart without even trying. She had tried to hold aloof because he must surely succumb to Tina's loveliness. Now, at least, she could be thankful that he stood in no such danger. But still he was not for her. She was grateful for Marianne's warning, though she earnestly hoped that it had been dropped by chance and not because she had betrayed herself. In self defence she had hastily devised the first criticism that she could reasonably level at the man who far too frequently invaded her thoughts.

She could not even have said when first she had begun to sense the truth. It had certainly not been a case of love at first sight! And though he had been kind to her since, had taken her part against Tina and shown himself sympathetic to her tastes, when had she first discovered that it was not just his sympathy and his kindness that she craved? She only knew that when other gentlemen became assiduous in their attentions she had found herself comparing them with his lordship and then, rather ashamedly, treating them with an undeserved coldness; pleasant mannered young men whom she had liked very well at a distance. One had tried to steal a kiss — and had his ears boxed for it.

Because it was generally known that her expectations were small, she was spared the attentions of the gazetted fortune hunters. For that she was grateful. It must be horrid to be courted for one's money. Just as horrid, she thought shyly, as being pursued because one was the son of a Duke. But even without the attraction of wealth she could have taken her choice between three or four gentlemen, respectable matches all, if not precisely of the first stare. What ailed her, then, that she must find them all insipid and boring when compared with a certain astringent gentleman who was not likely to concern himself with the insignificant Miss Forester?

It seemed as though her mind was to be schooled to thoughts of marriage that day, for the subject was raised again at the dinner table. Mr. Newton, dining at home for once, was in unusually benign mood, essaying one or two mild pleasantries on the infrequency of these cosy domestic evenings and vowing that he had not seen either his wife or his daughter for a sennight at least and his niece only at the breakfast table. This remark might have goaded his daughter into sharp retort, reflecting as it did upon her own less energetic habits, but fortunately she was not listening, being deeply absorbed in contemplation of the costume she meant to wear to attend a military review. Mrs. Newton said placidly that when they removed to the country at the end of the month he would soon be complaining that he could never escape from chattering females. They discussed one or two arrangements connected with the closing of the town house and Mr. Newton then turned again to his niece, declaring that he could scarcely believe she was so soon to leave them and inviting her in the kindest way to travel with them into Dorsetshire. "I believe you would enjoy it," he assured her. "Very pretty scenery, and you would be company for this wilful little puss of mine who always complains that there is nothing to do in the country."

This alluring prospect did not tempt Alethea to snatch at the proffered treat. She thanked him politely and, she hoped, with some semblance of regret, but explained that she was needed at home. Mama and Susan were to spend a month in Worthing in the hope that the sea air would be beneficial to Mama's health. To Alethea would fall the responsibility of looking after Papa in their absence.

Uncle Matthew commended her sense of filial duty, brushing aside her protests that it was no such thing, that she and Papa would also make holiday, after their own fashion.

"Poking about in musty old churches, I suppose," jibed Tina, who had emerged from her abstraction in time to resent her father's remarks about filial conduct.

"If you had some equally unexceptionable interest, you would not be forever complaining of boredom," returned her father severely. He turned again to his niece. "But how does it come about, my dear, that out of all the gentlemen who have been so ardently paying court to you these weeks past, you've not found one to outshine your Papa? For well I know there was more than one trying to fix his interest with you."

Alethea blushed scarlet. For once she had cause to be grateful to her cousin, who drew her father's fire by saying languidly, "Perhaps the gentlemen required rather more in a wife than just proper notions of filial behaviour. For my part I can imagine nothing more boring than a female who is for ever prosing on about duty and principles."

This speech had the double effect of bringing sharp rebuke upon the speaker and putting an abrupt end to Uncle Matthew's genial mood. With the skill of long practice, Aunt Maria initiated a discussion on the concert that they were to attend that night, and Alethea's matrimonial prospects were not mentioned again.

Unfortunately the concert proved to be rather mediocre, and Alethea, who was not particularly fond of music, found her thoughts straying with distressing frequency either to Marianne's confidences or to her uncle's teasing and from these to a consideration of the married state in general. There could be no comparison, for instance, between the marriage of her own parents and that of Uncle Matthew and Aunt Maria. Yet Aunt Maria was considered to have made a very good match while Mama was thought to have thrown herself away. Alethea could perfectly well imagine Mama keeping faith with her beloved for four weary years, just as Marianne had done, because she truly loved Papa. No considerations of wealth or social aggrandisement could so bind people together.

A patter of polite applause, signifying the end of an item, broke across her reverie, and she must rouse herself to take her part in the chorus of praise and criticism. But in the subdued mood induced by her reflections she was quieter than usual so that even Aunt Maria enquired if she had the headache. The two of them were alone in the carriage, the indefatigable Tina having gone on with friends to another party when the concert ended.

Alethea sat up hastily. "Just horridly mopish," she said lightly. "And quite without cause, unless it is that I have been spoiled by too much gaiety. Perhaps it is the prospect of going back to workaday life that is making me feel so low."

Aunt Maria took her seriously. "My dear child!" she said kindly. "I do hope you are not refining too much upon your uncle's remarks at dinner! He was only funning. There is nothing in the least derogatory about coming to the end of one's first season without having formed an eligible connection. Moreover your parents most particularly requested me not to press the matter. They wished only that you should acquire a little Town bronze — as the saying goes. But if you wish to make a push to establish yourself creditably," she went on in thoughtful tones, "I believe John Chester could be brought up to scratch with very little effort on your part. Or even Sir Evelyn Crowley, though he" — she broke off doubtfully.

Her horrified niece hurriedly disclaimed any matrimonial designs on either of these worthy gentlemen. "And indeed, kindest of aunts, can you not understand how much I shall miss our shopping expeditions, and our comfortable gossips after parties? Not to mention the balls and assemblies and theatres that I have so much enjoyed."

Aunt Maria was satisfied. Naturally, any girl suddenly realising that she must bid farewell to such delights was bound to feel a little low. She hastened to comfort the afflicted one with promises of a long visit to be paid next spring.

Perhaps because her thoughts had been so much with Marianne, Alethea was not particularly surprised to receive a note from her the following day. Recognising the handwriting, she tore it open eagerly, for surely it must bring news of James Borrodaile's return.

So, indeed, it did. James had landed safely at Spithead four days ago. Thence he had posted to Greenwich where he might claim hospitality from his kinsman and patron, the Governor. There were certain duties, certain enquiries into the welfare of former shipmates that could best be carried out from there. And at this final delay, Marianne had reached the end of her long patience. See him she must, however briefly, however formally. But alas! Mama was unwell. Nothing serious, the doctor said, just a slight chill, but she must keep her room for a few days. The thought of taking an abigail as chaperone was intolerable. Would her dear Alethea consent to forego the splendours of the military review and go with her instead to Greenwich?

Alethea saw nothing odd in the suggestion. Completely unversed in the rules governing naval and military procedure — it never occurred to her as strange that after serving so long in a beleaguered fortress, James could not snatch so much as a couple of hours leave of absence to come up to Town himself and visit his promised wife.

Nor had she the least notion how much pains it had cost Damon to coax his cousin into agreeing to the scheme. It had taken James's support — James, who had reached London shortly before noon and was, despite his weariness, benevolently disposed towards all mankind — to win her consent to such a deception. Imposing on her dearest friend! Even if the bit about Mama *was* true. But Damon felt that a journey by river to Greenwich would provide him with just the kind of situation that his present need demanded. James would be relied upon to see to all the trappings. If he could not borrow some kind of ship's boat and a well-trained crew from one his navy friends, then he had fallen sadly short of the standard required of the Marines. The river trip, Greenwich Palace itself, with its beauty and its historic associations, were just the thing to appeal to Miss Forester. As for deceit and play-acting, he was not asking a great deal. If Marianne could not feign a touching reunion with her betrothed, and that without undue effort, he wouldn't give much for their chance of a happy married life. Marianne, laughing, protesting, allowed herself to be overborne, and her letter was written at their bidding.

Alethea did not think that she would be missed from the large party that was to attend the military review. She was a little disappointed, since it so chanced that she had never witnessed such a spectacle, but the claims of friendship must come first. She dashed off a hasty note to Marianne, promising to be with her early next day. She naturally assumed that Kit would be their escort. He would scarcely desert his sister at such a time. Hetty promised that the note should be sent off at once, and Alethea hurried down to dinner to explain her change of plan to her aunt.

Mrs. Newton, much interested, agreed that her defection from tomorrow's party would cause no inconvenience. Of course she must go with Marianne. And Kit was perfectly to be relied upon to see her safe home again. If there was a gleam of satisfaction in Tina's lovely eyes for the new arrangement, no one particularly noticed it. Tina behaved very sweetly, wondering if the long-standing friendship between Marianne and James would now end in marriage, and promising to excuse Alethea's absence, if anyone should enquire about her, without betraying the mission upon which she was engaged.

Tina had good cause for satisfaction. Kit was being tiresome, hanging about her with reproach writ large in face and bearing. To have both him and Alethea removed for the day would make it just that much easier to spend most of her time with Damon. She had actually begun to wonder if his lordship had scruples about taking her away from Kit. Quite absurd, of course. She had never encouraged Kit in the belief that she might marry him. But how else could one account for the reserve with which Lord Skirlaugh treated her? He showed no such reserve in his dealings with Alethea. Of course he regarded her as a child, talked to her about such boring things as old battles, long dead kings, and the shockingly revolutionary ideas which had caused the rebellion of the American colonies. Just the kind of subjects that a gentleman might fall back upon when driven to converse with one who had no idea as to how to set about conducting a light flirtation. Tina, herself a mistress of that delicate art, thought he must be heartily sick of all this edifying talk, and just as thankful to be relieved of Alethea's presence as she would be of Kit's.

Chapter Eleven

Even when she was a very old lady, more than half a century later, Alethea could remember with crystal clarity every detail of that perfect summer day. She had but to close her eyes to see again the fringed parasol that she had carried to protect them from the sun's brilliance, the sheen on the hide of the grey gelding that Kit was driving when he called for her — very early, since Marianne had said that they must set out by ten. She had begun the day with the happiest of anticipations, planning with innocent cunning how best she might tactfully remove herself from the society of the reunited lovers, and wondering what topics would be most likely to divert poor Kit from his melancholy.

It had been a considerable surprise to learn that they were to make the journey to Greenwich by river, and, even as her eyes lit with delight at the suggestion, to discover that their escort was not, after all, to be Kit — for whom she had been at such pains to devise distraction — but Lord Skirlaugh. Her surprised face drew a gentle explanation from Marianne.

"Going by boat was Damon's idea. He chanced to be with me when — when I heard of James's arrival," she improvised hurriedly. "It was he who suggested that you might be willing to bear me company in Mama's place." And that, at least, was truth, she breathed thankfully. "He thought you would like to visit so historic a building, and that, since James was able to put a boat at our disposal — a cutter, I believe it is called — that you would enjoy the novelty of a different form of transport. That was why I had to ask you to be here so shockingly early. It seems that at this hour the tide will serve us well. Did *you* know that Thames had tides? I vow that *I* did not, until Ja — Damon explained it to me."

Alethea smiled for the slip of the tongue. It was plain that Marianne was bemused by her happiness. Useless to expect sensible conversation from her. She could think only of James. And her own heart was joyous. How kind! How truly kind of his lordship to take thought for *her* pleasure when he must be deeply preoccupied with his own affairs. Briefly — as she had done so often since Marianne had let slip the fact that her cousin had at last chosen a bride — she speculated as to the unknown girl's identity. But such thoughts, she well knew, would only give her a heart-ache. Resolutely she banished them. It was utterly foolish. There would be a price to be paid. But at least today was hers, and she would enjoy it to the full.

The circumstances, so different from anything in her experience, conspired to lend a dreamlike enchantment to the journey. The cutter was so immaculately clean, with polished brass and gleaming paintwork. There were even cushions placed in the sternsheets for the comfort of the passengers, plump square cushions, covered in blue and piped with silver cord. So very different from the wherries that Londoners were accustomed to use when they wished to cross their river. The sailors, too, in their picturesque clothing, sturdy and sun-tanned and smelling of soap and flannel and tobacco, and never so much as glancing over their shoulders to see where they were going. It was easy to imagine oneself as a princess of olden days, travelling in the royal barge from Westminster to Greenwich. Beside her, Damon, who had begun by pointing out various interesting features of the busy river scene, fell silent, sensing her mood and, to some extent, sharing it. On his other hand, Marianne was happily lost in blissful dreams of her own. The three of them seemed to be drifting in a fantasy world. The glitter from the dancing water that made even a parasol inadequate protection and forced one to half close dazzled eyes, heightened the effect. It was with a sensation of coming back from some far country that Alethea put her hands into Damon's and allowed herself to be helped ashore, and fortunately she was still too bemused to notice that the greeting between James and Marianne was surprisingly restrained for lovers who had been so long parted.

Indeed, after one brief irresistible peep to see what kind of man had won Marianne's heart, it seemed only courteous to avert one's eyes until such time as the pair had so far returned to earth as to have time to recall such mundane matters as formal introductions. Alethea turned her gaze to her surroundings and was at once entranced. The river frontage of the Palace was quite the most beautiful sight she had ever seen. Damon briefly indicated the salient features — the King's House, to her right, where the Governor had his quarters; Wren's graceful twin domes, and King William building where later, he promised, he would show her the magnificent Painted Hall.

They had strolled a little apart from their companions as they talked, but at this juncture Marianne called to them and she and James came up, hand in hand like a couple of children and full of laughing apologies for their casual behaviour. James was presented to Alethea in form, but it emerged that he and Damon were old acquaintances. Shipmates, in fact, though only for a very brief period. Alethea looked puzzled until James explained that marines served on board ships as well as ashore and that he had met Damon as a newly appointed and — he threw in, with a grin — painfully efficient first lieutenant.

James was one of those people with whom one was immediately at ease. He treated Alethea with perfect courtesy but as naturally and simply as though she had been Marianne's sister. It was not long before she was asking his advice as to how she should address the Governor. Never having met anyone so awe inspiring as an Admiral before, she confessed to certain nervous qualms. James smiled — an attractive flash of white teeth in his thin brown face — and told her not to trouble her head. Sir Hugh was perfectly amiable and much enjoyed the society of pretty mannered young females. A few questions about the establishment — the progress of the repairs to the Chapel, or the distinctive uniform of the pensioners — and the thing was done. On such topics he would discourse at length.

"*You* are the dangerous guest," he teased Damon. "Don't let him stray into Navy talk, and above all, don't mention the name of Keppel. He has never accepted the Court Martial's findings on that disastrous affair. But he's not likely to steer into troubled waters with ladies present," he consoled the girls, who were looking a little alarmed by these mysterious warnings.

In fact, luncheon passed off very pleasantly. Their host, while attentive to the comfort of all his guests, was naturally more interested in James and Marianne, and talk ran safely enough on their future plans. Alethea, a little over-awed by her surroundings and by the state which the Governor kept, sat drinking it all in, storing up memories to be savoured at leisure. Her patent appreciation pleased the Admiral who addressed several very civil remarks to her and regretted that he could not, himself, do the honours of the establishment as he had to attend a Committee meeting of the Directors. His guests deplored this circumstance with expressions of regret that were, alas, purely perfunctory. Sir Hugh might make an admirable guide, but three of them felt that they would do very much better without him, while the fourth — Alethea — was still fearful of the thunderbolts that she might bring down upon her if she was betrayed into uttering some tactless remark about the Navy or Courts Martial. Better to risk the insidious if far more dangerous sweetness of strolling about the lofty, elegant rooms, the courts and colonnades, the beautifully laid-out gardens with his lordship. Never out of sight of James and Marianne, of course, but generally, with kindly tact, out of earshot.

It was small wonder that of late Alethea's friends had found her unnaturally inclined to cling to Marianne's skirts, or, failing that shelter, even to Tina's, despite that damsel's manifest annoyance. To avoid Lord Skirlaugh's society entirely was impracticable, but as soon as she realised the danger in which she stood, she had done her best to set him at a distance. When that deep voice softened to warmth and gentleness, the crooked smile lightened the harshness of his normal aspect, she might feel as though her very bones melted, as though she longed only to give him whatever would bring him solace and contentment. But that wild sweet elation that flooded her being at his nearness should have no chance to swell to an irresistible current that could only sweep her away to bitter desolation.

Now they were flung together in virtual isolation. And if Damon had known the state of her feelings and deliberately chosen his venue, he could have found no better way of disarming her. His appreciation of historic places was as genuine as her own, and because of its naval associations, Greenwich was especially dear to him. In explaining the lay-out of the various quarters and in dipping haphazard into the past to recall memories of those who had known the Palace when it was in every day use as a royal residence, he forgot himself and even, for a while, his especial purpose in arranging this encounter. And his animation, his eagerness that Alethea should share his sentiments, drew the two of them together more delicately, more surely than any carefully rehearsed speeches.

By the time that their wanderings had brought them back to the Painted Hall Alethea's guard was down and they were exchanging views with their earlier freedom and candour. She gazed about her, awed to momentary silence as much by the magnitude of the display as by its artistic merits, and as usual her first comment was a question.

"Who painted it?"

"Sir James Thornhill — a well-known mural painter of Queen Anne's day. The ceiling of the Upper Hall is dedicated to her. This one" — he indicated the central oval of the Lower Hall — "as you see, is for William and Mary. The idea of a hospital for seamen was Mary's, you know, inherited from her unfortunate father. It is sad to think that she did not live long enough to see her plan become reality. See the inscription." He indicated the Latin phrases around the frieze.

Alethea, no Latin scholar, spelled them out slowly. "At least her husband gave her all the credit," she pointed out.

Damon nodded. "Yes. He pushed ahead pretty quickly with the building, too, considering his other preoccupations. It was to be his memorial to his beloved wife, so it was given precedence."

Alethea shrugged. "A chilly kind of loving. Poor Mary! I daresay she would rather have married one of her own countrymen and stayed quietly at home. Poor, lonely homesick little girl!"

"I doubt if queens have time to be homesick," suggested Damon bracingly.

"Do you? Of course she was homesick. She was only fifteen — a year younger than Sue — when she had to leave everything that was dear and familiar for marriage with a man nearly twice her age, who spent most of his time campaigning and left her to deal as best she might with a rigid court etiquette. And you doubt if she was homesick?"

She sounded quite fierce about it, thought Damon amusedly. "Royal personages are trained from childhood to acceptance of such marriages," he reminded her. "It is part of the price that they pay for their state. And if I remember aright, Mary learned to love her William quite devotedly. Why else should she have gone to the pains of creating an Orangery at Hampton Court? Surely that is the kind of sentimental gesture that indicates true affection?"

Alethea considered that carefully, then said, "For my part, I think her dairy is far more typical of her than a lot of silly orange trees in tubs. I see her as a housewifely creature who delighted in cleanliness and good order. It was her misfortune that she was born to royal state. She would have been far happier tending some comfortable manor and seeing to her lord's comfort when he came in weary after a long day in the saddle. As for William — if he had spent more of his time at home he might have got himself an heir, and so spared us" — and broke off short, scarlet-cheeked at the enormity of what she had said. Through her agonising embarrassment the thought came crossly, that was the worst of talking with his lordship. It was so interesting, so comfortable, that one simply spoke one's mind without reserve — and see what came of it!

But Lord Skirlaugh was feigning a convenient obtuseness. Not for worlds would he imperil, by so much as a raised eyebrow, the easy intercourse that he had so painstakingly sought. Moreover, his quarry had quite innocently led the talk into channels well suited to his purpose. So he said only, carefully, "Yes. A pity. A pity, too, that the little Duke of Gloucester died so young. But though you may have a romantic fancy for the Stuart succession, you will acknowledge, as did Aunt Emily, that we go on pretty comfortably under King George."

She seized thankfully upon his subtle twist to a delicate topic, denying, with unnecessary fervour, any leaning towards Jacobitism, and agreeing that, despite her affection for the things of the past, she was thankful enough to live in modern times. Her hot cheeks cooled. And his mention of Lady Emily gave her cause to enquire if he meant to make one of the party that was to drive out to visit her the following week.

This outing had been arranged on Tina's insistence, and promised to be a dashing affair. Closed carriages were unthinkable in summer weather, and landaus, decreed Tina, were 'stuffy' in the other sense. Curricles were the thing. In fact she had with difficulty been dissuaded from the notion of making the excursion into a race. Only a fortunate remark from Marianne, that, while she might be able to wind *Kit* round her finger, it was highly unlikely that *Damon* would approve of such hoyden tricks, persuaded her to draw in her horns. But it was to be quite a large party, since, in Tina's experience, large parties tended to pair off and go their chosen ways. Naturally they would not all inflict themselves on Lady Emily. Only a select group would be accorded that privilege. But the others could amuse themselves very happily in strolling about the grounds.

Damon now pointed out that there would be an extra man. Marianne could not be expected to go without James, who would naturally wish to pay his respects to his future bride's formidable relative. "In which case, Miss Forester, I shall beg of *you* to accept the seat in my curricle."

She said sedately, "It is very kind of you, my lord, but do you not think" — she hesitated, then pushed on bravely, "From some chance remark that was let fall, I had the impression that it was my cousin, not Marianne, who was to ride in your carriage."

Damon's brows lifted a little. "Miss Newton does me too much honour," he said softly, and would have liked to express his opinion of that young lady's encroaching ways with some acerbity, but the trouble in Alethea's face gave him pause. No doubt the poor child's life would be rendered miserable if the spoiled beauty did not get her way. "Then I shall at least hope to enjoy your company on the return journey," he said crisply, and when she did not immediately answer, said persuasively, "Come, now! Consider the possibilities of an encounter between your cousin and my aunt!" Her lips twitched in involuntary amusement. He said cordially, "Precisely so. I cannot help feeling that after an hour of such — er — stimulating exchanges, we shall be quite exhausted. If I do not have your promise to sit beside me on the return journey to soothe my jangled nerves, I shall certainly cry off from the whole affair."

She was staring at him now in steady enquiry. There was undoubted determination beneath the playful words, and though he was smiling a little there was an intent look in the grey eyes that she had never seen before. Unaccountably her heart began to beat a little faster and she could feel that she was blushing. She pressed the back of one hand to her warm cheek and said shyly, "You leave me no choice, sir." Then, drawing herself very erect, "Though your manner leaves me in some doubt as to whether I should thank you for your kindness or dip a humble curtsey and meekly promise to obey your commands."

His whole face changed as he broke into soft laughter. How he liked the imperious little tilt of her chin as she delivered her rebuke. What a wife she would make for a man who set considerable store by proper dignity and conduct! He bowed deeply, a stately reverence, and taking her hand in his raised it lightly to his lips.

"Forgive me, ma'am," he beseeched, the humble words belying the laughter in his eyes. "Desperate circumstances demand strong measures. I plead justification, and promise to conduct myself with the utmost humility next Tuesday if you will but give me the pleasure of your society."

This was a game that two could play, and Alethea was swift to seize the opening that he had given her. "Why, surely, sir," she said lightly. "I had only to think of Lady Emily's disappointment if you did *not* make one of our party, and there could be no doubt as to my decision. But the opportunity of studying your notions of humility will certainly add considerable interest to the occasion."

The grey eyes flashed wide. "Why! You naughty little thing, you! *What* a comprehensive set-down! And so sweetly, so kindly delivered. My congratulations, Miss Forester. I salute an adversary worthy of my steel. But look to yourself in future."

Alas! She would need to do so. This sort of heady exchange was no diet for a damsel already far sunk in love. It was the kind of play that should end in a close embrace and kisses. Punitive kisses — or so one pretended

— but none the less warm and sweet. And she longed only to yield to such punishment. But he was not for her. The words were becoming almost a battle emblem to which she must cling for survival. She looked about her for James and Marianne, but they had abandoned the painted deities and drifted out into the sunshine again, absorbed only in themselves.

"Shall we follow them?" enquired Damon, and she agreed thankfully, feeling that the presence of other people, real life, every day people, would help to steady her unruly heart. But in the gardens the pair were nowhere to be seen. Damon, having caught a glimpse of a familiar coat sleeve vanishing round a corner, had taken care to steer his charge in the opposite direction.

For on Damon, too, that brief crossing of swords had had a powerful effect. It had brought home to him the realisation that marriage with Miss Forester might not be just the staid, sober partnership that he had envisaged. Rather it seemed to hold promise of laughter and gaiety. That look of demure mischief on the girlish face when she had spoken of Lady Emily's disappointment! It had been no random jibe. She knew very well what she was about. He had been strongly tempted to catch her in his arms and make her pay forfeit for her impudence in kisses. Most certainly he would not waste the few precious moments of privacy that now remained to them in mere sight seeing.

"I was most interested in your views on royal marriages, Miss Forester," he began carefully. "From the masculine point of view I had thought that if a man offered his wife a position of great dignity and the power to do much good, housed her sumptuously and gave her everything that a reasonable woman could desire, then he might justifiably expect her loyalty and affection in return, even if the pair had met only briefly and formally before the marriage took place. *You*, on the other hand, seemed to find such marriages pathetic — even tragic. Why?"

Alethea considered her answer well. Marriage was a dangerous topic for discussion, even if it was limited to the marriages of long dead historic personages. "I did not condemn *all* such marriages," she reminded him. "Some of them may have been perfectly successful. But in general I do not think a marriage can be truly happy unless the contracting parties are deeply attached to each other from the outset."

"You sound very confident," he said shrewdly. "I think you have some particular marriage in mind."

She nodded. "My parents. They are — oh — it is difficult to explain! And of course one cannot compare ordinary folk with royalty. No considerations of state compelled them to marry. They did so because neither of them is really complete without the other. They are of one mind. Though by that I do not mean that they agree about everything. They were used to argue quite fiercely before Mama took ill, but it always ended in laughter. And can you not see already that James and Marianne will make just such a marriage?"

"And that is the kind of marriage for you?" he asked, deliberately keeping his tone light. "You would never consent to the other kind — the worldly kind — not even if Prince Florizel himself were to offer you the half of his kingdom?"

But Alethea thought the conversation was becoming much too personal. She had no desire to discuss her own marriage with this, of all gentlemen. Her tone matched his for light amusement as she replied, "What an improbable suggestion! Besides, the Prince Charmings of the story books always fell in love with the lady before making that very rash offer, which quite spoils your argument, my lord, since we were discussing marriages in which love had no place. As for a match of great worldly consequence — I stand in no danger of temptation! You should ask that question of my lovely cousin!"

"You under-rate yourself, Miss Forester, indeed you do. I, for one, infinitely prefer your society to your cousin's, as I made abundantly plain not a quarter of an hour ago."

What more he might have said was unfortunately lost, since at that moment the Admiral himself, with James and Marianne, was seen approaching. There was no further opportunity for private conversation, but on the whole Damon was not dissatisfied. His appreciation of Miss Forester's personality was growing apace, and although, in his view, she set too much store on love, at least it was on a steady and enduring love, not the idealistic romantic passion which most girls of her age seemed to think so desirable. It should not be difficult to persuade her that love, of the kind that she valued, would come naturally after marriage. And at least she could no longer be in any doubt as to his intentions, and she had not hinted him away as he had given her every opportunity to do. At the next opportunity he would suggest that he would very much like to meet her parents. That would put everything on a proper footing. In happy ignorance of the true state of his chosen bride's feelings, and with a growing conviction that matrimony — when one became accustomed — might be quite enjoyable, Damon went contentedly to bed and slept soundly.

Alethea, after a shattering scene with Tina, who had come home early from the review in a furious temper over Damon's defection and refusing to believe that her cousin had not deliberately contrived the whole thing, was also thankful to escape to the shelter of her bedchamber. Tina's parting remarks echoed in her ears as she rather wearily submitted to Hetty's ministrations.

"Do you imagine he'd look twice at *you*? A dab of a girl with no claim to beauty and countrified to boot! Unless he's heard of Cousin Albert's will — and I wouldn't put it past you to have let fall a hint about *that*, sly scheming wretch that you are."

Well — she had not let fall a hint — had never dreamed that Cousin Albert's money, even if were doubled and trebled would buy her an offer from Lord Skirlaugh. Nor would she want one, on those terms, she thought proudly. Relaxing gradually to the caress of the cool sheets, she carefully rehearsed all that had been said between them, weighing every word, so vividly remembered. If she had not known, thanks to Marianne, that his affections were already engaged, she might almost have imagined — But that, of course, was because she would have liked to imagine it. She dwelt blissfully for a little while on the thought that at least he preferred her society to Tina's, wondered uneasily how she could maintain an attitude of cool detachment in the intimacy of a drive a deux in a curricle, and finally drifted into uneasy dream-haunted slumber.

Chapter Twelve

"I daresn't, miss. I'm right-down sorry but I just daresn't. I'm not clever nor quick like gentry folk, even if me mam did say me dad was a gen'leman born. I'd make a mull of it as sure as eggs is eggs. And if I was caught it'd be the jail at least if it wasn't transportation."

"But I was relying on you, Toby. You said you would do *anything* for me. Not once, but several times you swore it. And this is such a small thing. I can't do it for myself because I don't understand about carriages, but *you* could do it so easily. Please!" Tina's eyes were great beseeching pools; her mouth drooped pathetically.

The lad's face crimsoned, an ugly, dull flush which sorted ill with his sandy hair and pale blue eyes. But the eyes returned Tina's gaze squarely, though he licked his lips nervously. "Yes, miss. I know I did. But I meant anything in the line o' duty, and me not wanting to be paid for it. Meddling with a gentleman's carriage is different. Even if I could do it — which I don't say as I couldn't, 'cos there's 'alf a dozen different ways o' making a ve-hickle break down haccidental-like and no one to know no better — 'oo's to say what would come of it? A break-down's one thing, but it all depends where it 'appens. Say you're goin' at full gallop and a wheel comes orf. That's nasty, that is. Might be someone killed. You'd not want aught like that to 'appen, all along of a bit o' mischief, would you now, miss?"

Tina hesitated. What Toby said was common sense. And certainly she had no wish to suffer injury in a carriage accident. But she had made up her mind to a certain course of action and she would not permit wiser counsels to prevail. Lord Skirlaugh apparently admired a girl who kept her head and behaved coolly in emergency. Very well. He should see that Miss Newton could play the part to admiration — even if she had to contrive an accident to prove it to him.

"There'll be no risk of anything more than an awkward spill," she told the boy serenely. "I shall see to it that the carriage is travelling at a very moderate pace. If *you* can contrive that a wheel shall come off, I will do the rest. We are to lunch at the inn at Hampton Wick, so you will have no difficulty in approaching the carriages, and you know Lord Skirlaugh's curricle well enough to avoid any risk of tampering with the wrong one. If anyone should question your presence there, you may say that you have an urgent message for me. I will even furnish you with a letter to be delivered to me. I really don't see what can go wrong."

Toby could; a great many things. Yet Miss Tina was depending on him. She had said so. He remembered all the dreams he had woven about serving her. How he had rescued her from blazing buildings, sinking ships (despite the fact that he could not swim) and villainous abductors; and now he was reluctant to perform the simple service that she asked of him. But she didn't understand what it meant, bless her innocent heart. To her it was just a bit of naughty mischief — a set-down for Lord Skirlaugh because, she said, he was so conceited about his driving. If it had been a phaeton, now, he wouldn't have minded so much. Mebbe, in that case, there'd be little harm done, unless his lordship was springing 'em, which wasn't his usual way. Besides, Miss Tina had said she would ask him to drive slowly. But a curricle! A two-wheeler — and could be on a busy road with other vehicles involved and Miss Tina in the midst of it. No! He would rather endure her scorn and disappointment than put her at such risk, even though he burned to show her how cunningly he could have done the job.

He had no idea how easily the astute maiden watching him with those big appealing eyes could read the conflicting feelings mirrored in his irresolute face. Well she knew that scolding would not serve. At his sullen rejection of the whole affair she permitted herself just one reproachful glance before she lowered those devastating lashes. "Oh, Toby! And I had thought you truly my friend," she said sorrowfully, and turned dejectedly away.

"No, miss! Wait!" exclaimed poor Toby, tried beyond his seventeen-year-old strength. And then, as she glanced back over her shoulder, jerked out, "All right, then. I'll do it, if so be as I can," and, still hoping to dissuade her, "Only what'll I say to the master? For 'e's an ill man to cozen and 'e'll want to know why I'm takin' the day orf."

Tina was not in the least interested in this aspect of the affair, but she was well aware that her ally was still wavering. "Could you not say that you felt unwell?" she asked plaintively. "Or perhaps that your mother was ill and that you must go and see her?"

Toby did not think the owner of the livery stable would be impressed by either of these improbable fictions. "More likely to turn me off without a character," he said glumly.

"If he does, I shall persuade Papa to engage you as my own particular groom down in Dorset," Tina assured him.

The lad stared at her incredulously. "D'yer really mean it miss?" he breathed, his eyes beginning to glow with excitement.

"Indeed I do. I can't think why I haven't done so already, for no one understands my wishes as you do. But you must do *your* part first you know, and so contrive that his lordship's pride and his superior person take a tumble in the dust. How will you manage it?"

Poor Toby! He was just sufficiently green just sufficiently infatuated, to believe her pretty promises. His scruples were swept away in the medley of joyous plans for a rosy future in which he would always be near Miss Tina, always her faithful servant and protector. He thrust out his meagre chest and smiled at her.

"Easy enough," he said confidently. "I can fix the linchpin so's it'll 'old for 'alf a dozen miles. 'E'll not know nothing's wrong till it goes and the wheel comes orf. But mind you do what *you* promised, miss, and make 'im take it slow. Else it 'ud be proper dangerous, see?"

Tina promised, and returned to the patiently waiting Sophie, the young French maid who had taken Hetty's place. Sophie thought the ways of English demoiselles were very odd indeed. An assignation with a gentleman she could understand, but what could miss want with talking so long to a common stable boy? The pair continued their stroll in the Park, the picture of demure innocence.

She had managed that very neatly, thought Tina complacently. They would be leaving Town in a week's time and quite out of Toby's reach if he thought to pester her about her share of the bargain. She had a sudden picture of her father's face should she ever venture to suggest that he employ an uncouth youngster whom he would unhesitatingly describe as the scum of London's kennels. It was so comical that she almost laughed aloud. The only nuisance lay in the fact that she would be obliged to patronise another livery stable next season. But perhaps by then she would be a married lady. The courage and calmness that she planned to display could not fail to impress his lordship. He would realise that there was more to her than her beauty, her charming manners and a substantial portion. The thought of his admiration sent her home in a mood so sunny that, after the thunder clouds of the past three days, the whole household relaxed thankfully.

Alethea set out on her second visit to Hampton Court with very mixed feelings. On the one hand she looked forward with pleasure to renewing her acquaintance with Lady Emily and to spending her day in such delightful surroundings. On the other she dreaded the awkward scene that must ensue when Tina discovered that Damon intended to take *her* as his passenger for the return to Town. The cousins had scarcely exchanged more than a dozen words since the day of the military review. Even if they *had*, Alethea doubted if the circumstances would ever have been propitious for such a disclosure.

But by the time that the actual moment of confession was upon her, she could only be thankful that a disastrous afternoon was approaching its end. The day had begun pleasantly enough, save for the weather which was oppressively hot. Tina was in her gayest mood, driving off with Damon in the wake of James and Marianne. Alethea's own escort was the young hussar officer who had sprung to her defence when Tina had snubbed her so unkindly at her début party. He confided almost at once that he had a great ambition to become, as he phrased it, a 'first-rate fiddler'. But as he then added that he believed the foundation of such success must lie in establishing a good understanding with his horses rather than in attempting feats of showy whip-work that were at present beyond his skill, she was able to enjoy her drive in comfort, to refrain from drawing his attention to a charming view just when he was negotiating a sharp bend, and to talk horses with unfeigned interest at such times as he could spare a little of his attention for the social niceties.

But the afternoon was fraught with discomfort from the moment that they were admitted to Lady Emily's private apartments. It was difficult to say just why. Tina's company manners did not usually put one to the blush. Perhaps on this occasion she was a little *too* anxious to please, a little too conciliating. She addressed Lady Emily with a deference so marked as to be slightly suspect and, in general, treated her as one who must be cherished and tended with such care as one bestows upon the near senile. It was an attitude that did not take at all with Lady Emily. Remembering the very different treatment that *she* had been accorded, Alethea could scarcely credit the malicious humour with which her ladyship proceeded to expose her cousin's every weakness.

She voiced several ridiculous and even contradictory opinions and nodded pleased approval as Tina echoed them with sycophantic enthusiasm; led her, by artfully innocent questions to acknowledge a lack of principle quite shocking in any female with claims to gentility and displayed her to her embarrassed fellow guests in the worst possible light. She might, perhaps, have wearied soon enough of this one-sided pastime. One, moreover, which she would undoubtedly have condemned in any other hostess as being a shabby way to treat a guest. Unfortunately, before the novelty had had time to pall, she had turned to Alethea and suggested that she might care to show her young escort some of the glories of the State Apartments. "and I could not put you in the hands of a better cicerone," she assured him graciously. "It is quite amazing how much history the child knows."

It was at this point that Tina chose to echo and improve upon Lady Emily's sentiments. "Deplorable, is it not, ma'am?" she said lightly, patronisingly. "My little cousin is never so happy as when she is poking about some musty old building or has her nose glued to letters and diaries writ by persons who would not have had the time for them if their own lives had not been so deadly dull. Mama is quite in despair over her. Says it is high time she left the schoolroom behind and directed her thoughts to more profitable matters."

Lady Emily herself had advised Alethea to much the same tune, if rather more kindly. But she had liked the girl at that first meeting, even to the extent of mildly regretting that she had no fortune to recommend her as a possible bride for Damon. To have this spoiled, conceited chit decrying her was more than she could stomach.

Alethea and young Gilbert could do no other than fall in with their hostess's suggestion, though Alethea had already seen enough of Lady Emily's methods to render her deeply uneasy. Gilbert's, "Phew! Regular old termagant, ain't she?" did nothing to allay her fears; and the atmosphere upon their return, after a very cursory tour of the main points of interest, confirmed that the worst had happened. Lady Emily looked smug, Tina complacent. But Marianne's hunted expression and James's quizzical one betrayed all too plainly how the game had gone. Only Damon appeared to be unperturbed, though after one swift glance at Alethea's face he took the opportunity afforded by their interruption of removing his aunt's prey from her clutches.

"With your permission, ma'am, I would like to show Miss Newton something of the Palace. You are behaving very badly, you know, devoting your whole attention to her, when here is Marianne's betrothed anxious to improve his acquaintance with you. Come, now! Yield her to me for a little while. As yet she has seen nothing of her surroundings."

Their eyes met and clashed, slow amusement in Damon's, guilty defiance in Lady Emily's. But hers were the first to yield. "Very well, then," she said crossly. "Be off with you, if you must. Though in my day a fifteen mile drive from Town would have given a young man opportunity enough for all that he needed to say. And don't keep her out too long."

Tina positively preened. To have Damon claiming her society and Lady Emily bestowing such distinguishing attention upon her was just what she had hoped for. She smiled bewitchingly at Damon as she set her hand upon his proffered arm, promised Lady Emily in dulcet tones that they would not be gone above half an hour, and allowed herself to be escorted from the room.

"Half an hour!" snorted Lady Emily disgustedly. "What does she hope to see in that time?"

Since no one ventured a reply, she added on a more reflective note, "At least the boy has too much sense to let himself be trapped by *that* piece of brass-faced perfection." She turned to Marianne. "Has he made up his mind yet? Found a wench who fulfils all his exacting requirements?"

"So I believe, ma'am," returned Marianne primly. But when the old lady plied her with eager questions she would say only that it was the merest speculation and that to be discussing her cousin's private affairs so openly must be embarrassing to their friends. Recalled to a sense of decorum, Lady Emily rang for her maid, directed that cakes and wine should be brought for the refreshment of her visitors, and, as though purged of all malice by her recent spirited performance, addressed herself to James in the kindliest way. Since Damon had the good sense to keep a very willing Tina strolling about the ancient walks for a good deal longer than the prescribed half hour, the remainder of the visit passed off comparatively peacefully, until Lady Emily announced her intention of coming into the forecourt to watch her guests drive away.

"I've always had an eye for a good bit of horseflesh," she announced complacently, "though it's long enough since I used anything but stolid hirelings. I sometimes think you can judge a man pretty well by the cattle he keeps and the way he handles 'em."

106

The remark was scarcely calculated to reassure her male guests, but worse was in store for the ladies. Having stumped round the three vehicles with the support of her ebony cane, delivered a highly critical opinion of the assorted steeds, and told Damon that it was time he bought a new curricle, since, in her hey-day, no girl with any pretensions to fashion would have consented to ride with him in that shabby old thing, she turned her attention to her own sex. Open carriages or not, she told them severely, they would not have been permitted to go jauntering about the countryside without so much as a groom in attendance if they had been in *her* charge. Nor did Marianne's timid reference to the sizeable group of friends whom they were appointed to meet in Hampton Wick serve in any way to placate her. Was a vehicle never known to fall behind its consorts, she wanted to know. Or to take a wrong turning, or a so-called short cut?

Having triumphed over Marianne, she relented enough to say that perhaps in her case it was allowable, since she was driving with her affianced husband, then fixed Tina with a penetrating stare and enquired in whose company *she* had made the journey from Town.

"In Lord Skirlaugh's, ma'am," returned that young lady. And then, in the serene belief that she was already established in Lady Emily's regard, added saucily, "Unlike you, ma'am, I don't disdain to ride in a shabby vehicle when its owner is so accomplished a driver and so agreeable a companion."

Damon turned away to hide his amusement, and made pretence of adjusting a buckle as he recalled the commonplace exchanges that had earned him this encomium. But Lady Emily was outraged. The brazen hussy, to dare to speak to her in so familiar a fashion! She said coldly, "Then certainly you must return with someone else. You cannot spend the whole of the day in Skirlaugh's pocket without causing undesirable comment."

Tina was nonplussed. To affront Lady Emily by disobeying her was more than she cared to do. It would be to jeopardise all that she felt she had gained. But what of her plans?

While still she hesitated, Damon said smoothly, "You are very right, Aunt Emily. I should have thought of that for myself. Perhaps Miss Forester would be willing to change places." Secretly he could have hugged the old girl for making his way so easy.

Tina was still a little loth to abandon her carefully conceived plan, though during the past hour she had begun to wonder if it was, after all, quite so clever. What if she were to suffer some hurt? Serious injury was unlikely if they were travelling slowly enough, but even minor abrasions might leave her temporarily scarred. Worse still, she might break or lose a tooth! Besides, in view of Damon's attentive solicitude during their stroll in the Palace grounds and the way in which he had coaxed her to stay with him long after the prescribed half hour, perhaps it was not, after all, necessary to proceed to such extreme measures. No doubt Lady Emily's attitude had helped him to make up his mind. She made up hers. Alethea should take her place on the homeward journey — and the risks that went with it. She didn't wish her cousin any particular harm, though the thought *did* just cross her mind that it would be better if it was Alethea who lost a tooth. Alethea's were whiter and more even than her own.

The day, which had throughout been a little too hot for enjoyment, was now definitely sultry. The sun had vanished behind a heavy overcast and livid clouds were massing ominously in the south east. The gentlemen consulted earnestly together in the inn yard, interrupted only when one of them offered Tina a letter, which had, he said, been brought by 'that lad from the livery stable'.

Tina bit her lip. How like Toby to allow himself to be not only seen but recognised. She accepted the letter nonchalantly.

"Stoopid fellow was hanging about the stables," volunteered the bearer. "Can't think why he didn't come up to the inn. Couldn't have expected to find you in the coach house."

But it was clear that he saw nothing suspicious in the circumstances and turned away at once to join the argument as to whether the road by Strawberry Hill and Twickenham was preferable to the more direct route over Putney Heath. It was longer, but it offered more possibilities of obtaining shelter should the threatening storm break. Opinions being divided, the party split up. The little party who had visited Lady Emily were the last to leave. Tina heard Damon suggest that they follow the more direct road and promptly begged young Gilbert to take the other one. She did not know whether or not Toby had managed to achieve his purpose, but she meant to be well away from the scene of any possible accident.

"May have to put 'em along a bit if we're not to get a wetting," said Damon cheerfully, easing his pair up Kingston Hill, "but I'll not press them at this stage."

Alethea agreed to it, thankful for the flow of air that cooled her burning cheeks, and presently gathering courage to ask apprehensively, "Did Lady Emily pursue her — her — *baiting* tactics the whole time?"

He chuckled. "She did. Most successfully. I dared not catch James's eye. It was the funniest thing I've heard in months. Now don't look like that, child. It's no bread and butter of yours. Your cousin has a dozen times your experience. Only her overweening conceit blinded her to traps that should not have deceived a child. *You* are not to blush for *her* folly."

That was true, of course, but Alethea found it very lowering just the same. It was no pleasant thing to be made a laughing stock. She could only hope that Tina would remain in happy ignorance of the figure she had cut. She sighed sharply.

He was swift enough to sense her mood, and as the horses reached the crest of the hill and broke into a gentle trot he spoke of other things. She responded sensibly enough but without her usual animation. He ventured the suggestion that at least the threat of coming storm might protect them from the threat of hold-up on the Heath. That made her smile a little and beg an explanation of his reasoning.

"Because the gentleman of the road would reckon on poor pickings in such weather," he explained, urging the horses to a canter. "This storm is coming up faster than I anticipated, Miss Forester, and we are driving into it. With your permission, I'm going to spring 'em."

The curricle might be a trifle shabby, but it was well designed. His lordship's horses were beautifully matched, and with those capable hands holding the reins there could be no question of anxiety. Surrendering to the intoxication of speed, Alethea's spirits rose. This was delightful. She found herself wondering, rather reprehensibly, how soon they would overtake the vehicles that had started ahead of them. It must be almost at once, for his lordship was maintaining a splitting pace, but so far there was no other carriage in sight.

There was a sudden spatter of large raindrops. She put up a hand to brush them from her cheek, heard a sharp crack that sounded like a shot, and immediately called to mind the highwaymen of whom they had been talking. She looked up, half expecting to see some sinister masked figure, pistol in hand. Instead, she saw a wheel bowling rapidly down the road. She was still staring at it, wondering where in the world it had come from, when the curricle swerved violently all across the road, lurching heavily as Damon fought to check the headlong pace, and ending on its side in the off-side ditch, decanting its two passengers without ceremony on the rough verge.

Chapter Thirteen

Alethea's recollection of subsequent events was never very clear. When first she was fully conscious of her surroundings she was tucked up snugly in her own bed with a dull headache, a streaming cold and Hetty in attendance. She could scarcely believe it when Hetty told her that two days had elapsed since that eventful visit to Hampton Court. Hetty said that she was not to worry, that she would remember all about it eventually. It was just because she had struck her head against something or other when she was thrown out of the carriage. To anxious enquiries about Lord Shirlaugh, the maid gave soothing replies. He had sustained no serious injury, had, indeed, called in Berkeley Square that very morning to enquire after his fellow sufferer, though he was still limping heavily and walking with a stick. She then announced that her patient had done enough talking and must now swallow the potion left for her by the physician, close her eyes and rest.

Alethea was very willing to obey. But as she drifted in and out of periods of semi-consciousness and drugged sleep, fragments of recollection came back to tease her. She could still see that wheel bowling down the road. It seemed to spin on for ever before her aching eyes. There was a memory, too, of being soaking wet and very cold and of someone struggling rather clumsily to wrap her in a coat; of her own voice crying, "Don't go! Please don't leave me!" She slept again, and presently roused with the scent of sweet hay in her nostrils. She must have been dreaming. But what a queer thing to dream — that she had been lying, cramped and stiff but warm, clasped in Damon's arms, with the sweet smelling rustling hay all about them. Her head ached too much to puzzle it out. She slept — more deeply this time — and woke to find her father sitting beside her.

She struggled up on one elbow in her delight at seeing him, to be pressed gently back against the pillows and told to lie quiet while he kissed her cheek and patted her hand and bade her not to be anxious for everything was quite all right.

She could see no cause for anxiety — save that Papa had left home at an inconvenient time to visit a daughter who ailed no more than a throbbing head and a disfiguring cold — but she accepted his soothing words as an expression of affection, and having been assured that Mama had withstood the shock of hearing about her accident with great fortitude, relaxed drowsily on her pillows and listened to his news of home. He could not stay long; must, in fact, return that night. He had thought to come up to Town again in a day or two to escort her home, but since she seemed to be going on quite prosperously he might not put himself to the trouble, since Aunt Maria had said that Hetty should go with her.

"I just wanted to tell you myself that Mama and I perfectly understand how it came about. It was an accident, and no possible blame can be attached to you. Lord Skirlaugh himself explained the circumstances to us in a perfectly straightforward fashion. I liked that young man. You were extremely fortunate to be in such good hands. So just make haste and get well quickly, for you will have a great deal to do in these coming weeks."

His expression was grave and he spoke with unwonted earnestness. Alethea was puzzled, for how *could* she be held to blame for the accident? But she was still a little hazy from the effect of the medicines that the doctors had prescribed and it never occurred to her to seek another interpretation of Papa's words. Then Hetty came in with a cup of broth for her patient, and Papa rose to take his leave, thanking Hetty for the care she had given his little girl. Alethea supped her broth and eased her aching limbs and wondered why neither Aunt Maria nor Tina had been to enquire how she did. Tina's neglect was not, perhaps, unexpected, and Aunt Maria must be very busy with all the preparations for removal to the country in addition to her other engagements, but surely she might have found two or three minutes to visit her afflicted niece. But perhaps she *had* done so, and she herself had been asleep at the time.

When she enquired of Hetty, that discreet personage only primmed up her mouth and "couldn't rightly say." It was obvious that she could say a good deal if she so chose, but she contented herself with reminding Alethea that the doctor had said that she was to be kept quiet and had straitly forbidden all visitors. Alethea felt a vague sense of discomfort. Could she, in some way, be in disgrace with her aunt? The accident must have caused a good deal of extra work and possibly some small anxiety, but it was not like Aunt Maria to take a pet for something which was not really her fault. She lay and puzzled over this strange behaviour until sleep claimed her.

Morning found her much restored. Only Hetty's firm insistence kept her in bed until the doctor had called. Fortunately he was pleased to say that she might get up for a little while during the day, though she must guard against over-exertion and lie down upon her bed if there was any sign of the headache returning. No sooner had he departed than she pushed aback the coverlets and climbed rather gingerly out of bed. On the whole, she supposed, she had escaped pretty lightly. She wrinkled her nose at the mirror, which showed a pale, peaked little face with a spreading yellowish purple bruise above the right temple. She rather thought she would stay indoors for the remainder of her sojourn in Berkeley Square! She had no wish to flaunt *that* doleful visage about the town.

Hetty, returning from escorting the doctor downstairs, exclaimed indignantly and shooed her back to bed. "And there you'll stay, miss, like a sensible girl, till you've eaten your luncheon. Hebe 'n me's got it all made up to dress you between us, and Hebe to do your hair so's it'll partly hide the bruise. Your aunty says you're to receive his lordship in the Green Saloon."

Alethea stared. "Receive his lordship? Do you mean Lord Skirlaugh?"

Hetty looked guiltily conscious. She tried to carry it off with a high hand. "Why, who else, miss? Hasn't he called each day to enquire for you? The mistress said you was to see him as soon as the doctor gave permission, and mightily thankful she would be when" — She broke off short, aware that her tongue had run away with her.

"Thankful when *what*?" said Alethea slowly, sure now that something was very wrong, something that she did not understand. And when the maid did not immediately answer, "Thankful when I am gone?" she queried sorrowfully, "So much trouble as I have made?"

That brought Hetty to startled life. "No, miss, she never!" she gasped in convincing indignation. And then, quite unexpectedly, grinned. "It's my belief your aunty would have been well enough pleased with the way things've fallen out," she confided, "if it hadn't been for Miss Tina kicking up such a rumpus and neither fit to hold nor bind."

"But why?" begged Alethea, wholly bewildered. "She *cannot* be jealous, just because I was involved in an accident — or does she think that I contrived the whole thing on purpose to become the talk of the Town?"

There was the briefest possible hesitation. Then Hetty said slowly, "No, miss. She knows very well you didn't. Because *she* did."

Alethea put a hand to her head. That blow must have affected her brain. The girl *could* not have said what she had heard. But Hetty went on, "That wheel never came off of its own. Miss Tina had persuaded one of the lads from the livery stable to meddle with it. But his lordship being nobody's fool and finding this lynch-pin or whatever they call it had been near sawn through, nor it didn't match the one in the other wheel, began to make enquiries, and someone remembered seeing this lad hanging about the carriages. It all came out then. Give Miss Tina her due. She'd thought *she* would be the one riding in the carriage. Seems she'd taken a fancy to being a heroine. Your uncle was in such a taking as I never saw — said he'd never heard such a crack-brained notion in his life and she was only fit for Bedlam. He packed her off to her Grandmama the very next day, for all her weeping and cajolery. Told her she could be thankful Lord Skirlaugh didn't choose to lay an action against her. Her Mama went with her to see her safe to Hoddesden which is where old Mrs. Newton lives, and very retired, too, which won't suit Miss Tina. Hebe went with them — your aunty and her got back late last night — and says she is talking very wild. The last thing was that she'd decided to marry Sir John Boothroyd after all, because if there was one thing she couldn't abide it was the thought of you being married before her. But I shouldn't think that'll hold," she ended reflectively.

"Nor any need for such impetuous haste," said Alethea absently, her thought more concerned with assimilating the startling information that Hetty had disclosed, "since there is no immediate prospect of my marrying."

An odd expression crossed the older woman's face. She opened her mouth as though to say something further, thought better of it, and closed it again.

"So that is why Aunt Maria didn't come to see how I was. You might just as well have told me, Hetty. I had begun to imagine something quite horrid."

"But you'd not have been satisfied with half the tale," said Hetty shrewdly, "and I was on no account to talk about the accident. Now just you lie quiet till it's time for your medicine. Your aunty will be in to see you in a little while. She took breakfast in bed this morning. Tired after the journey, not to mention Miss Tina's sulks."

Despite Hetty's explanations and assurances it was a rather anxious face that Alethea lifted for her aunt's kiss when that lady made her tardy

114

appearance. To be sure she was in no way to blame for Tina's banishment, but she quite expected to find Aunt Maria in the lowest of spirits and to have to exert all her energies to soothe and cheer the poor lady, no easy task when one was feeling a little low oneself.

But it turned out to be no such thing. Aunt Maria was possessed of that happy disposition that can put unfortunate happenings quite out of mind as soon as the visible evidence is neatly tidied away. Tina had been very naughty, but she might safely be left in the capable hands of Grandmama Newton, and Aunt Maria could devote herself wholeheartedly to the much more entertaining business of guiding her dear little niece at this critical juncture of her affairs. Not that she anticipated any difficulty. Girls *could* take foolish notions into their heads, but not Alethea, always so sensible, so tractable. In which happy confidence the good soul trotted briskly into her niece's room and embraced her warmly.

By the time that Aunt Maria had exclaimed pitifully over the invalid's wan looks, recommended a soothing lotion for sundry part-healed scratches and expressed her gratitude to the Providence that had preserved both victims of the accident from serious and lasting injury, any lingering doubts were banished from Alethea's mind. Whoever might hold her in some way blameworthy — as Papa's consoling remarks had suggested — Aunt Maria's affection was as warm and unclouded as ever.

She settled down in a chair beside the bed and enquired with deep interest what dress the girl proposed to wear for the all-important interview.

Alethea stared. "I had not particularly thought about it. Is it *so* important? I thought his lordship was but paying a courtesy visit to enquire as to my progress. In fact I couldn't understand why I must receive him in solemn state in the Green Saloon. As for my dress" — she chuckled — "which do you think would best set off my unusual colouring?" And she pushed the hair away from her temples to exhibit the ugly bruise.

Aunt Maria shook her head reprovingly. One's appearance, one's dress, was never a matter for jesting. "I think the cream sendal with the apricot velvet sash will be the most suitable," she pronounced judicially. "It strikes just the right note of restrained elegance. Strong colour would only make you look paler, and though a little romantic pallor may be allowable under the circumstances, I would not wish his lordship to think that your constitution is sickly. Not but what he would still have to offer for you.

However, you are a sensible girl and will understand that he has also to consider the succession."

She broke off to consider it, with deep and patent satisfaction. Her dear little niece to be a duchess some day. One could not condone Tina's behaviour, of course, but really things could not have fallen out more fortunately!

Every vestige of colour fled from Alethea's face. Her eyes looked enormous — dazed. It was a full minute before she could master her whirling thoughts, control her voice to say, with some semblance of calmness, "Do you mean that Lord Skirlaugh intends to make me an offer? Is *that* what he is coming for?"

"But of course, my dear. What else?" returned her aunt complacently. "He drove down to Tunbridge Wells the very next day to seek your Papa's permission to pay his addresses. Everything of the most correct. For all their quiet ways, the Byrams are very high sticklers. But *you* will not object to that. And from what your uncle says, your Papa took quite a fancy to him. Your Mama was naturally a little overcome by so much excitement, and was not able to receive him. But it was at his suggestion that your Papa travelled back to Town with him so that he could see for himself that you were going on comfortably and reassure your Mama. I daresay that was what raised him in Clement's estimation, for such thoughtfulness, you know, augurs well for his character as a husband."

She elaborated happily on the qualities that went to make a good husband, all of them, she was sure, to be found to a marked degree in Lord Skirlaugh's disposition, quite unaware that her niece did not hear a word, being wholly preoccupied with the task of reducing her own chaotic emotions to order.

Why should she feel nothing but dismay upon learning of his lordship's intentions? A few days ago such a prospect would have brought only rapturous anticipation. What was wrong? First Papa, then Hetty, as she now realised, had been well aware of the situation. Suddenly she recalled Aunt Maria's carelessly turned phrase. 'He would still *have* to offer for you.' That was it! It was not because he loved her, but for some other reason. Perhaps he blamed himself for negligence and felt responsible for the accident. But that was ridiculous!

Forgetful, for once, of the demands of good manners, she cut across her aunt's rambling discourse to say crisply, "Yes, ma'am, I daresay his lordship *is* truly amiable. But why did you say that he would still have to offer for me even if I was of a sickly habit?"

Aunt Maria stared at her in frank surprise. "But my dear child! Of course he must do so. Perhaps your memory is still a little clouded. I know it was so when they brought you home — indeed, I believe you were scarcely conscious. But *his* recollection was perfectly clear, and even had he wished to repudiate his obligation to you he could not have done so, for you were seen, you know."

Alethea was feeling more and more bewildered, but she was determined to solve the puzzle. "Who saw us? And when?" she demanded.

"Why several people, I believe," said Aunt Maria, puzzled in her turn, but anxious to be helpful. "There were the Ingesters. His lordship had you carried to their house as soon as he was able to summon help. And *they* sent for their doctor, so he saw you, too, of course. But I am sure they are all perfectly to be relied upon not to tattle. And the others who saw you were quite inferior persons who either would not dare or would not be believed. Don't look so anxious my love. The announcement of your betrothal will make all smooth, I promise you."

"But what is there to tattle *about*?" demanded Alethea desperately. "Surely there is nothing shameful in being involved in a carriage accident?"

Her aunt stared again, then broke into an indulgent smile. "I see you *don't* remember," she said. "Even if you did, you are such an innocent little puss that you would scarcely credit the significance that evil-minded persons might read into your little adventure. My dear, it was *not until next day* that his lordship was able to summon assistance. What with the storm, so that there was no one about, and his own injuries, which made it impossible for him to walk, it was as much as he could manage to get you to shelter. Indeed, your uncle vows that his efforts must have been positively *heroic*." Her voice dropped to a conspiratorial note. "But the fact remains, my love, that you spent the whole of the night alone with him in the Ingester's hay barn. Of course he must marry you. You would be utterly ruined else."

Chapter Fourteen

Lord Skirlaugh, calling in Berkeley Square punctually to the appointed hour, was received by a young lady outwardly composed, inwardly distracted to breaking point by her own conflicting feelings. Aunt Maria had reasoned, argued, pleaded, scolded and finally wept at finding her gentle biddable niece irrevocably set on a course that could only bring *her* to social ruin and make life extremely uncomfortable for her family. Alethea remained unmoved. She was truly sorry that her conduct should bring discomfort upon her kind aunt but, she pointed out soothingly, they would be removing from Town almost at once and by next season it would all be forgotten.

"Scandal is *never* forgotten," said Aunt Maria gloomily. "Just when you think you have lived it down it rears its ugly head again. You are ruining Tina's chances you know, as well as you own."

With true nobility Alethea refrained from pointing out that in that case Tina would be well served. "Any girl as lovely as Tina will always have chances," she said gently.

"If only she would hold by her determination to marry Sir John," sighed Aunt Maria, momentarily diverted. And then, perceiving another line of attack, "But if you persist in bringing scandal upon us all, I daresay he will withdraw his suit."

"Not if he truly loves her," consoled Alethea. "As for me, surely you would not have me marry where there is no love, just to satisfy convention?"

"The love would come after marriage," urged her aunt eagerly, proffering the familiar placebo as though it were wisdom fresh-minted. "And you would have a position of the first consequence. Think how well suited you are — your principles — your tastes — oh — it would be the happiest of marriages, I promise you!"

If only they would leave her alone to think things over calmly! If only she knew more about the girl whom his lordship had planned to marry! Perhaps he was only substituting one marriage of convenience for another which had suddenly become more necessary. If that was the case, why not accept the suggestion that love would come after marriage, snatch at the chance that was offered her, and make the best she could of it afterwards? In the recesses of her troubled mind she heard a voice — it might have been Papa's — say quietly, "Because it would not be an honest bargain."

At that her aching heart flared into passionate resentment. "Perhaps not. But it is I who would be the loser by it. I would give all my heart in exchange for dutiful kindness. Oh, yes! He would be kind. His pride would ensure that I was well treated. A hollow mockery of the warmth of love that can permit two people to argue and differ and squabble and yet be so truly one that they can laugh at themselves as they do it."

"Love can be an embarrassment, a heavy burden to a decent man, if it is given unasked," said the voice dispassionately.

But they gave her no peace — no time to refute that argument — to settle in her own mind what was best to be done. They never left her alone. Aunt Maria, Hetty, Hebe, neither of whom dreamed that she would refuse so magnificent an offer. Each in her own way brought pressure to bear. The two abigails, not knowing of her dilemma, fretted her with their assiduous attentions. They were careful not to mention the expected caller or his business, but their barely suppressed jubilation as they went about their duties all too plainly betrayed their knowledge. Wearily she allowed Hetty to fuss over her with a cup of supporting broth, question which slippers she would wear, sprinkle her handkerchief with scent; agreed that Hebe might curl her hair, "Just this once, miss, to help hide the bruise." By the time that she was dressed and ready to go downstairs to the Green Saloon ("I chose it especially, because it is on the ground floor and would spare his lordship the trouble of climbing the stair with his bad leg," Aunt Maria had said reproachfully) she had not been allowed so much as five minutes for quiet reflection. She felt more like a mechanical puppet with a set part to perform than a living, breathing girl, and the headache that the doctor had warned of had returned in full force. Yet if she admitted to it, the whole thing would be to face again. Better to go through with it now and have done.

She seated herself in one of the elegant gilded chairs which were a feature of the room and gazed blindly at the pages of a journal which Hetty had thoughtfully placed in her hands until the sound of the door bell, followed almost at once by the approach of halting footsteps set the colour flaming briefly in her white cheeks. Then, as Ponting announced her visitor, the painful colour subsided and she steeled herself for what she must say.

Alas! In her miserable turmoil of indecision, she had not allowed for Damon's injuries. He did his best to minimise the limp, little dreaming that it served him far better than his normal free-striding arrogance, but he had resigned his stick into Ponting's keeping, feeling it to be slightly incongruous to a proposal of marriage, and walking without its support was both painful and difficult. So Ponting was able to report, to such of the domestic staff as he judged worthy of the confidence, that miss had flown to meet her lover like a bird to its mate.

If the butler's sentimental heart had caused him to slightly overstate the case, it was so far true that Alethea had briefly forgotten her own anxieties in her concern to install her visitor in the only comfortable chair that the room offered. This he accepted and sank into gratefully, though he declined her further offer of a footstool to raise the injured limb, saying gravely that he was not yet so far sunk in decrepitude. He was a little amused by her solicitude, but it seemed to him an odd way to welcome a suitor. Was it possible that Miss Forester was unaware of his purpose?

Then he saw the suddenly downcast eyes, the quivering lips, and promptly absolved her of all duplicity. She knew. And she had acted in innocent good faith at sight of his awkwardness. Poor child! Small wonder that she was embarrassed. *This* was not how he had planned to woo her.

He said wryly, "We make a pretty pair, do we not? And all thanks to your ingenious cousin! You have been told the whole tale of it, I trust, and will absolve me from the crime of negligence where your safety was concerned?"

"Yes, indeed, my lord," she returned gravely. "And though I remember very little of the events that followed, I understand that I have to thank you for getting me to shelter before I had caught my death of the lung fever. That, at least, is my maid's view of the case. And Uncle Matthew describes your efforts in my behalf as truly heroic."

"Your uncle exaggerates," he said curtly. "You have little to thank me for. In fact I daresay it was my curst clumsiness that caused you to suffer so many bruises and scratches. The physician whom the Ingesters summoned asked if you had been dragged through a quick-set hedge. The thing was, you see, I could not walk and I had to get you into shelter somehow." He laughed, though ruefully, at the humiliating memory. "Believe me, ma'am, a man loses much of his self esteem when he can no longer go upright. I made what shift I could, but I fear you were dragged to that barn rather than carried. It was, perhaps fortunate that you were barely conscious."

"Was that when you put your coat on me? For I do remember that."

"I thought it might afford you some protection. That bank seemed to be entirely given over to thistles and brambles."

The thought of his care for her induced a strong desire to throw herself into his arms and burst into tears. Deliberately she fought it down. "It seems very odd that no one came to our assistance. That is usually quite a busy road."

"We were singularly unfortunate," he explained — his phrasing unfortunate, too, in the circumstances. "The storm came up very quickly. Such vehicles as might have been on the road had sought shelter, for the rain was a positive deluge, the thunder and lightning almost tropical in their intensity."

"And no habitation in sight? No belated labourer homeward bound?"

He was apologetic. "None, ma'am, to my vast regret."

Were ever words so innocently spoken more ill-chosen? He had been thinking only of her comfort and safety, of the soaking she might have escaped. To Alethea they conveyed only his bitter distaste for the situation in which he found himself.

But at least the sting of them braced her failing courage. "So you carried me to this hay barn, where we sheltered until morning," she said bluntly, anxious, now, only to have done with this painful interview.

There was a sudden, taut silence. Then he said levelly, "Yes, ma'am. Which is one reason why I have called upon you this afternoon. I had intended to wait until you had returned to your own home before approaching your Papa for permission to pay my addresses, but the circumstance you mention rather forced my hand. It would be idle to deny that it might give rise to malicious speculation, speculation that would be distasteful to both of us. It therefore seemed best to post into Kent forthwith and acquaint your parents with the whole story. Your father was so good as to approve both my action and my plea. Miss Forester, will you do me the honour of accepting my hand in marriage?"

She heard him out patiently to the end, her eyes lowered, her lips pressed tight together to conceal their traitorous trembling. If only she could say, "Yes." He was doing it so kindly, trying to convince her that he had meant all the time to ask for her instead of, as he put it, having his hand forced.

She was all the more determined that he should not suffer for his generosity.

"My lord, you do me great honour," she said steadily, if a little huskily. "I regret that my cousin's folly should have put you to so much trouble in my behalf and am deeply appreciative of the great kindness you have shown me. But I do not believe there is any need for such extreme measures as you suggest. Whatever the appearances, we are both of us wholly innocent. I do not see why we should be pushed into matrimony merely to satisfy convention. So I thank you from my heart for your very obliging offer."

You could always rely upon Miss Forester to take an unexpected line, thought Damon, divided between exasperation and amusement. Though he scarcely knew what he *had* expected. Certainly not a refusal based on the principle of resisting coercion! But somehow, although he could not help knowing that society held him to be a matrimonial prize of the first order, he had *not* expected her to drop willingly into his arms at the first time of asking. He looked curiously at the tightly composed little face and wondered how best to set about persuading her to see things in a different light.

"I must ask you to bear with me a little longer on this head," he said politely. "Your cousin's meddling, the attitude of society, did not *prompt* my proposal. They only caused it to be made rather prematurely. So could you not bring yourself to ignore those factors? At least encourage me to hope that if I am patient a little longer, as I had meant to be, you will give me a different answer."

This was unbearable. He was behaving so beautifully, almost convincing her that he really meant it, though well she knew that it was only his chivalry. Not daring to trust her voice, she shook her head dumbly.

"No? Yet I had thought we were good friends," he said persuasively. "Have you not enjoyed the hours we have spent together? To me they have been delightful. I have felt that we had a good deal in common and would suit very well."

There was no help for it. Somehow she managed to force a choked little voice out of her desperation. "My lord, I *cannot*."

He stiffened. Slowly the old bitterness crept back about his mouth. The grey eyes were bleak. "I see," he said, his voice suddenly so harsh that she was startled out of her own misery and stared up at him, uncomprehending. "Do you know, I had actually forgot? Of course you could not contemplate marriage with so grotesque a caricature of a man. You can give him your pretty smiles, your animated interest, as you have done so generously. But marriage is different, isn't it, Miss Forester? Not even to save your good name could you bring yourself to conquer your repugnance."

The sheer injustice of the bitter words was the last straw. Alethea's hard-held control snapped at last. She forgot all about proper conduct and maiden modesty and sprang up from her chair in a fury that out-matched his own. Before he could rise, hampered as he was, she had set both hands on his shoulders and half shaken, half pushed him back into his chair. "Do you think I would care for a few paltry scars if I loved you?" she flared at him. "How dare you insult me so? You're *obsessed* with your scars. No one else notices them one half as much as you do. If *I* were your wife, I'd be proud of scars so nobly, so bravely won. *This* is what I'd do to your silly old scars!"

Her hands released his shoulders and came up to frame his face, their touch gentle, now. She tilted his head so that the scars were fully exposed, noting, almost impersonally that a new, jagged cut, deep and angry looking had been added to them, and then stooped and gently kissed his cheek, smoothing her lips lightly and tenderly over the seared and puckered skin.

For a long moment they rested so. Then, as fury faded, realisation dawned, and she sprang back, her hands going to her shamed face as she half sobbed, "Oh! What have I done? Please, oh, please, don't tell Aunt Maria." And then, with a touch of her usual spirit, "But you *did* provoke me so!"

There was an odd little smile from Damon for that. And shall do again, my darling, he thought; deliberately and often. But instinct warned him to tread warily. There was something here that he did not understand. And since, in the last two minutes, he had suddenly discovered not only that there was, after all, such a thing as true love but also that there was only one wife in the world who would do for him, it behoved him to discover why she would have none of him and set about mending matters.

"*I'll* promise not to tell Aunt Maria, if *you'll* agree to forget the foolish things that I said," he suggested coolly.

"Oh! Thank you! Yes. Of course I will," said Alethea, rather disjointedly, and still seemed to be poised on the edge of flight.

"Please don't run away," he begged, but lightly, easily, as though it was no great matter. He felt suddenly and fiercely alive, his mind working at racing speed, every faculty alert. "I promise not to distress you with further importunities. But even if you won't marry me, surely you would still *help* me? Are we not friends again?"

She assented to that, promptly if a little doubtfully. Friendship — with a man whom one loved to distraction — was like to prove both costly and painful.

"Then will you please consider my position? *My* reputation is just as much in question as yours. I will allow yours to be your own affair. But unless our betrothal is puffed off within the next few days, I shall be in ill-odour indeed. I shall be marked down as an unprincipled blackguard. Society will cast me out. No more invitations from careful parents. Young ladies will look the other way or plead previous engagements when I ask them to dance with me."

She was looking quite anxious, his funny little love. But she was no fool. Better not try her credulity *too* high, though the bubbling eagerness within him was urging him on to ridiculous audacity. He drew a solemn face. "You, if you were willing, could help me in this."

"Could I?" she said doubtfully.

"Why, yes. If I promise not to tease you with my attentions, would you consent to visit my parents at Byram? That would put my position in a much more respectable light."

"Would it?" — even more doubtfully.

"Why, of course it would!" This time that inner exhilaration ran away with him. "Everyone would see that I had done my best to make an honest woman of you. When no betrothal ensued, they would probably lay the blame on my father."

"But that would be wrong," she said simply, bewildered by his changing moods.

"Little my father would care! He's a great gun, for all his quiet ways. You'll like him, I think. My mother and Rachel — my sister-in-law — you must love. No one could help it. And Byram is beautiful at this time of year, with the corn ripening and the heather just coming into bloom. Please say you will come!"

She scarcely noticed that he was already taking her consent for granted. In this mood it was difficult to refuse him anything.

"I must go home first," she pondered. Then, more firmly, "Papa and Mama must be told the whole of this scheme of yours. Then, if they approve, I will come."

Chapter Fifteen

Everyone was so understanding, so helpful. Aunt Maria, having been favoured with a heavily expurgated account of the interview in the Green Saloon, decided that all was not yet lost. Privately she saluted his lordship's nerve in treating her niece to such a farrago of nonsense. As though the heir to a dukedom would ever be so ostracised! But the thing was that Alethea seemed to have swallowed it, and far be it from Aunt Maria to undeceive her. She commended the girl's decision to consult her parents, said that, for her part, she thought Alethea owed his lordship such reparation as lay in her power, and offered the services of Hetty to support her niece in the anxious business of staying with such exalted personages.

Papa listened to all she had to say, remarked mildly that he believed his lordship to have sound principles and a well-informed mind, but said that if Alethea did not feel that she was ready for marriage then her father was only too happy to keep his daughter at home for as long as she chose to stay. As for visiting Byram, she and Mama must decide between them what was proper. He could not help feeling that it would be a pity to miss so rare an opportunity. Byram was very old, very lovely. He was sure she would find much there to interest her.

Alethea, while wholly subscribing to this last remark, if from quite a different point of view, began to feel slightly hunted. She had expected Papa to be wholly opposed to the scheme and she felt that she needed either strong opposition or firm support to help her make up her own mind, for by this time she didn't know whether she wanted to go or not. Damon had insisted on driving her home, with Hetty to play propriety, pointing out that this would be the least that the interested would expect of him in the way of correct behaviour. He had also done a great deal more, driving down to the Wells twice to enquire how she did and on one occasion putting up overnight at the George and Dragon in Speldhurst in order to drive Mama out in the new phaeton with which he had replaced the wrecked curricle. His behaviour had been exactly that of a gentleman concerned to fix his interest with a lady. He brought her flowers, entertained her with the latest news of her London acquaintance, escorted her on a very prosaic household shopping expedition and strolled with her in the Rectory garden. But since she could not be sure whether he was sincere or merely play-acting, she was more bewildered than ever.

Mama — well — Mama had fallen in love with Damon, or so her husband declared, vowing that he had never seen such an arrant flirtation in his life. The day of Alethea's home-coming, Mama's chair had been set in the garden under the walnut tree for coolness. The two of them had come to her there, outlined against the blaze of a westering sun, so that she was dazzled and could see few details. Her first impression of Damon had been of a tall man, dark, and, she thought, very proud, despite the informality of buckskins and driving coat, who still walked with a slight limp.

Their first exchanges had been purely formal but when Alethea had been despatched indoors with the kindly suggestion that she should change her carriage dress for something cooler, Damon had looked full at his hostess and come straight to the point.

"Forgive me, ma'am, if I sound abrupt, but I have a good deal to say in a very short time. Your daughter is not one to dawdle over changing her gown."

She gave him a little smile for that, but her eyes were watchful.

"From what I have *not* said," he went on, "you will have guessed that there is no engagement between us. Miss Forester declined my offer on the grounds that she would not be pushed into matrimony just to satisfy convention."

"A very sensible reason," she observed seriously.

It was his turn to smile, though only briefly. "I should perhaps add, ma'am, that I mean to do all in my power to induce her to change her mind. With which end in view I have persuaded her, by slightly devious means, to visit my parents at Byram next month. She will tell you all about it herself, will, in fact, only consent to the visit if you and her father approve. What *I* want to say, ma'am, is, will you help me?"

She looked him over long and thoughtfully, and he endured the scrutiny patiently, never once thinking of a scarred face, intuitively aware that, like her daughter, this woman would see beyond the surface.

Presently she said quietly, "If I like you I will help. But it is early days to be sure. You love her?"

"With all my heart, ma'am," he said rather grimly. "But I was fool enough to discover it just too late. I proposed to her chiefly on grounds of suitability — common interests — shared principles — I daresay I need not enlarge on that head."

"But you did not tell her that you loved her."

"At that moment, ma'am, I was not aware that I *did*," he said, a note of exasperation creeping in.

"Ah!" she said wisely. "I see. It is because she refused you that you suddenly became so fond. Denied you, she was more desirable."

He swung round on her with what she privily described to her husband as a positive snarl of fury, then remembered that she was woman, a delicate one at that, and Alethea's mother. He said quietly, "I cannot blame you for saying it. It is what anyone might think. But it is not so. When Miss Forester refused me, I behaved very badly. I flung it at her that it was because of my scarred face that she could not endure the thought of marrying me. It made her very angry. She said — what she did then — it's no good, ma'am, I can't explain it sensibly, but it was like coming out of a dark prison cell full of nightmares and horrible imaginings into clean sunlight and cool air," he finished simply.

Mrs. Forester, who could imagine very well what her daughter had done and was becoming increasingly aware of a certain desire to imitate the shameless hussy's behaviour, said softly, "I see." Then, rousing herself to a slightly more militant attitude, added briskly, "There is just one more point, my lord. You have spoken of suitability — community of tastes and principles. You said nothing of rank and fortune."

The silence this time was uncomfortable. At last he said slowly, "I know we are not equals in rank. But we have been bred up in the same tradition of duty, integrity and service to our people. Would you punish me for being the son of a Duke?" And then, sensing her sympathy, went on audaciously, "We can none of us help our parents, ma'am."

The twinkle in her eyes reassuring him, he finished gaily, "As for fortune — well — there's no use denying my father would rather have seen me wed an heiress. You are a country woman, ma'am. You will understand that a place like Byram has a hungry mouth that is always in need of filling. But there are things of more value than money, and Byram may go short of the stuff for once. If I can persuade — *when* I persuade your daughter to marry me," he corrected, the black head tilting defiantly, "I shall be more than content. She has a gift above gold, even above rubies. How many women are there, do you think, who can give a man his faith again? A man bitter and disillusioned as I was. And not even because she loved me, but from innocent warmheartedness."

Mrs. Forester entertained some very strong doubts about that last statement, but the poor boy seemed to believe it, bless him. She said slowly, "It will not be easy. Speak to her, now, of love and she will not believe you. She will put it down to your noble nature, or some such folly."

"In any case I have promised not to pester her with unwanted attentions."

Mrs. Forester laughed, a soft gurgle of sound that made him smile in return though he could see nothing funny in what he had said.

"How *truly* noble!" she mocked. "But my dear boy, there are more ways than one of wooing a girl. I can see I shall have to take your education in hand."

"Then you will help?" he demanded eagerly.

"Indeed I will. To the best of my ability." She held out her hand, laughing up at him, and he clasped it firmly in token of alliance. Eyes brimming with mischief, she tugged gently at the captive hands so that he came, puzzled, to kneel beside her. Gently she put up her other hand to the crisp dark hair, tweaked it lightly, kissed the scarred cheek and said softly, "Do you think I do not know my own daughter?"

If Alethea had entertained any lingering thought of evading the Byram visit they were banished when the Duchess's letter of invitation arrived. Its tone was simple and friendly. She was invited to spend the whole of August with them. There was mention of a projected visit from Marianne and James during the latter part of her stay, which the Duchess hoped would add to her enjoyment of a quiet country holiday. And in her closing paragraph she suggested that perhaps Alethea's father would like to spend a week at Byram before escorting his daughter home again. She understood from her son that Mrs. Forester was not yet able for so long a journey, a fact that she much regretted. She would hope to have the pleasure of making her acquaintance at a later date, having heard so much about her from her son. Meanwhile their Chaplain at Byram would be happy to exchange pulpits with Mr. Forester if that would be helpful.

It would have taken a much harder heart than Alethea's to quench the eager delight that shone in her father's face at this proposal. There was no more talk of whether she should or should not go. Preparations were set in hand and all was bustle. Mama and a rather wistful Susan were comfortably established in their apartments in Worthing and Hetty packed Alethea's trunks for a month's stay in what Papa teasingly described as 'the barbarous borders'. Papa had shed twenty years in his anticipation of such a holiday as he had never dreamed of, and made even his rather half-hearted daughter laugh with his ridiculous, solemnly uttered warnings as to the customs obtaining in the north.

A suggestion that a good supply of flannel petticoats and warm shawls would be a great deal more useful than all those flimsy gowns that Hetty was folding so carefully might be heard with filial respect, even if disregarded, since Papa was a north-countryman by birth. But the offer of a chain-mail hauberk, his dearest treasure, to be worn beneath those same gowns for fear of border reivers and moss-troopers reduced her to helpless giggles.

Papa, however, seemed to feel that his high spirits had betrayed him into going beyond the line of what was pleasing, and reverted to his more usual manner. And this time his daughter was hard put to it *not* to laugh, for the reverent voice in which he recited the names of the towns through which she would pass on the Great North Road, "Stilton, Stamford, Grantham, Newark — names redolent of history! The very stones will speak to you," put her irresistibly in mind of the way in which he pronounced the Benedicite.

Chapter Sixteen

Papa was at least so far right in that Alethea enjoyed the long leisurely journey far more than she had thought possible. For the most part she travelled in that same carriage that had once served as an al fresco dressing room, Judd on the box, positively cheerful these days, since he found Hetty an entertaining sparring partner in their off-duty hours. Sometimes his lordship would join her for an hour or so; sometimes, if the weather and road conditions permitted, he would coax her to ride with him. The little brown mare, most inappropriately named The Mudlark, had been brought along for her especial use, if she chose to ride. A young groom, whom Alethea vaguely recognised, led her when she was not required and seemed to be responsible for her welfare.

The constantly changing scene, the exercise and the busy posting inns all helped to raise Alethea's spirits. Everything was fresh and novel. There was ample food for her lively curiosity. And in answering the many questions and pointing out the various places of interest along the way, it was not long before Damon was re-established on almost the old friendly footing.

Almost, but not quite. His behaviour was beyond praise. Her comfort, and Hetty's, was provided for in every detail, with a forethought that was as thorough as it was unobtrusive. When the two of them talked together he so managed it that the chosen topics were interesting, amusing, even controversial, but never personal. Yet despite his care, he sensed in her a wariness, a reserve that he could not penetrate.

Once, in a careless moment he betrayed himself. They had arrived betimes in Newark where they were to rest overnight, and he had persuaded her to stroll out with him to view all that remained of its castle. As they returned, she expressed her regret that they could not stay longer in the town, so much as there was to invite exploration. Quite unthinkingly Damon suggested that the next time they came that way she might stay for as long as she pleased. He saw her check in her strolling pace, then move on again, saying quietly, "You forget, my lord. When next I come this way,

I shall be with my father — and he will be in haste to get back to Mama and to his parish duties."

But arrived at Byram she lowered her guard a little. She was naturally shy, a trifle overawed, and Damon was an old friend among so many strangers. She could turn to him with confidence for any information necessary to her peace of mind and know that he would not laugh at her or despise her ignorance of the ways of great houses. So two weeks passed very pleasantly, and even the weather smiled upon them. There was no need for flannel petticoats, thought Alethea with a smile, though it was certainly much cooler than in Kent, a coolness that she found invigorating. They drove out to visit several beauty spots in the neighbourhood, rode together every day, and, on the two occasions when the weather was really hot, went boating on the lake. The Duchess apologised for not holding parties in her guest's honour, pleading laziness, which was manifestly untrue, and explaining that there would have to be parties when Marianne and James arrived and, with the weather so fine, it was a pity not to take advantage of it.

"We must have a picnic on the island before you go home," suggested Damon, careful not to fall into error again. "Edward and I were used to spend most of our holidays there when the weather permitted — and the grown-ups! We even built a log cabin there, so that we could sleep in it and play Robinson Crusoe. I wonder if it is still standing."

It was the first time that he had spoken to Alethea of his brother, and since he said no more and made no attempt to land on the island, Alethea judged that the pain of his loss was still acute. She knew from Lady Rachel that the two had been very close. Damon, the younger brother, adoring and copying the older one, Edward fiercely protective.

"Damon has never really forgiven what he felt was the throwing away of Edward's life," she had said sadly, "and when he failed in his brave attempt to save our son, his whole disposition seemed to change. He is more himself this summer than he has been since Edward's death. A happy marriage will, I believe, bring back something of the dear, lovable boy over whom we have all grieved so deeply."

This was coming too close. Alethea said rather stiffly that she sincerely trusted that his lordship would soon find a suitable marriage partner with whom he might achieve this felicity.

Lady Rachel did not appear to notice any withdrawal of intimacy. "I shall be so thankful, both for him and myself," she confided. "I cannot desert the Duchess, whom I dearly love, but my brother needs me so much more."

"Your brother?"

"Yes, my dear. His wife is so very frail. Indeed, we fear the end cannot be far away. The lung sickness, you know. And two small children — the youngest a mere babe. You can see how I am torn."

Alethea could. And her tender heart grieved for the sad little family. But it could not change her feelings about marriage with Damon.

It was not quite so easy to ignore the Duchess's remarks. The Duke, who did not employ an agent, preferring to keep matters in his own hands, generally vanished into the estate office after dinner. The rest of the party amused themselves with books and needlework or music and card games, as the mood took them. On this particular occasion Damon had gone off with his father. Rachel had been singing, her voice not very powerful but sweet and true. The song done, she remained at the piano, drifting gently from one melody to another, her fingers idling over the keys. The Duchess sat watching her for a little while before turning to Alethea to say, "I shall miss her so very much when she goes, but I think she will be happier with her brother. She dearly loves children and those poor little mites need her more than I do. I fear I have been selfish in clinging to her companionship for so long. But you and I go on very comfortably together, do we not?"

Alethea could only blush and stammer what she hoped were appropriate thanks and pretend to be unaware of the underlying significance of the pleasant words. Approval — acceptance — could scarcely have been more blatant. In one way it made her very happy. But when one felt bound to disappoint these innocent hopes, one felt the meanest of traitors. And the Duchess was such a dear. The sight of her anxious, loving eyes dwelling so tenderly on her tall son tore at Alethea's heart. She began to think gratefully of the impending arrival of Marianne and James. It would be easier when there were other guests to distract the attention of these lovable ladies from her guilt-stricken self.

Marianne and James were due to arrive on Thursday. There were but three more days to be endured. Surely she could hold out for *so* long against the gentle but inexorable fingers that were thrusting her into Damon's arms? For she still believed that her original decision had been the right one — and Damon had given her no reason to think otherwise.

On Wednesday night the Duke took a hand in the affair, telling Alethea over dinner that he had received a letter from her Papa and suggesting that if she could spare the time to come with him to the library after dinner, she might like to read it. But when he had settled her in a comfortable chair and told her that Papa hoped to arrive on Saturday, he made no attempt to give her the letter. Instead he said gravely, "My child, how does it come about that my son believes you to be practically penniless? Your father, feeling it to be his duty under the circumstances, informs me that you are, on the contrary, a very considerable heiress."

Alethea's head went up proudly. Duke or not, she could not see that it was any business of his. Then she remembered that he was also her host and Damon's father. She said with dignity, "My parents, your grace, did not wish me, in my first season, to be exposed to the attentions of fortune hunters when they could not be at hand to guide and advise me. It seemed to them wiser that word of my inheritance should not be bruited abroad. I naturally submitted to their wishes."

He studied her thoughtfully, a gleam of appreciation in the grey eyes so like his son's. So she had a temper. Good! And had it in control. Even better. He said quizzically, "There was no romantic notion of persuading my son to declare the world and wealth well lost for love?"

The blaze in the soft brown eyes quite startled him. By the Lord Harry, he thought, if she had a sword, she'd spit me for that! There was a long pause before a perfectly colourless little voice said, "No, your grace. Nothing of that kind."

Inwardly he saluted the child's demeanour. But since Damon had told him the whole, he must move carefully. "You relieve my mind," he said gently. "I had judged you to be above such romantical folly, and am thankful to have my opinion confirmed. Though if my son had known the truth, I might have been spared some extremely boring, not to say disrespectful homilies on the value that should be set on character and disposition as opposed to mere money. All of which I heartily agreed with before he began. Not that it spared me anything. However, I daresay you and he will settle the business best between you. I'm no hypocrite, Miss Forester. If you decide to marry my son, I won't pretend that your fortune won't be very useful. I *can* honestly say that I'd have welcomed you thankfully without it, since I think his happiness lies in your hands. Don't look so distressed, child. *I* won't tell him. Good night. Sleep well!"

Alethea could only be grateful for dismissal, since she was left without words. She slept very badly indeed — for a girl not yet twenty — and was wide awake by six o'clock. She had never left her room so early before, but she could bear inaction no longer. She put on her riding dress, moving softly to avoid rousing the sleeping Hetty in the adjoining room, and went quietly downstairs. The servants were already astir. A surprised abigail brought her a glass of milk and an apple and Bellamy, Damon's deerhound, came pleasedly to greet her. The huge creature had, from their first introduction, taken it upon herself to escort the visitor in all her comings and goings when her master was unable to do so. Only Alethea herself was unaware of the singularity of this behaviour. The entire household had noticed it with emotions that ranged from amused interest to downright awe, and it had done much for Alethea's prestige. Presently the two of them made their way to the stables. Alethea had been told that The Mudlark was entirely at her disposal — she had only to ask Belling to bring her out. She did so now. A brisk canter would at least distract her thoughts if it could not solve her problem.

In the event it actually underlined the problem, since Toby Belling seized the opportunity of begging her pardon for *his* share in the accident that he had helped to bring about. *Now* she knew why she had half recognised him. She must have seen him about the livery stables, though how he now came to be in Lord Skirlaugh's service was still a puzzle. He was only too eager to explain. But as his remorse, his gratitude for an inexplicable forgiveness and generosity, his adoration for his new master, spilled over in tumultuous and slightly incoherent phrases, she struggled anew to escape from those relentless voices that urged his lordship's claims. Here was a man worthy of any woman's love. Who was she, to demand that first he must love her?

James and Marianne were late. Alethea was already changing her dress for dinner when the soft, urgent tapping at her door announced her friend's arrival, and Marianne, glowing and breathless, came in. Her first exclamation was one of concern. "My dear — you look worn to the bone! What *have* you been doing? Oh dear! It will be very awkward if the air at Byram doesn't suit your constitution!"

At this point Alethea, recognising the signs, hastily dismissed an interested Hetty and assured her friend that she was perfectly well and happy to see *her* in such high bloom.

"Yes, I daresay," said Marianne quite brusquely. "But you, my love! What's amiss? Is Uncle Hugo being difficult? I was afraid of that. I have looked each day in the Gazette, hoping to see the announcement of your betrothal."

Alethea turned on her almost fiercely. "Would *you* accept a bridegroom because Tina's foolish play-acting had forced him to offer for you?" she demanded. "He doesn't really want me, certainly doesn't love me. You told me yourself that his choice was already made. Do you think me as selfish and greedy as Tina that I must snatch at the offer of high rank, just because sheer chance has flung it at me."

"But" — said Marianne. And stopped. She was horrified that a few careless words of hers should have caused such mischief. She, at least, would meddle no more. But Damon should have the truth of the matter before she slept that night. Hastily she fell back on woman's ever-ready excuse. "My love, I must change my dress. Uncle Hugo will be cross if we keep dinner waiting. We were dreadfully late arriving. One of the horses cast a shoe and the smith's fire was out. We can talk later," and fled.

*

"I don't know whether to hug you or shake you," said Damon. It had proved impossible to talk with him privately during the evening, since the newly arrived pair were the centre of attention, but Marianne, knowing that she would not rest until her confession was made, had taken the desperate course of going to his dressing room before he retired for the night. His expression of shocked incredulity had swiftly vanished at the trouble in her face, though he could not wholly check a speculative conjecture as to what his valet would think.

"Yes, I think it must be the hug," he decided thoughtfully. "To be sure, if you had not meddled — yes, yes, I *do* understand precisely how it came about, you need not explain again — we might have been betrothed by now. On the other hand I would certainly have missed a very rare, a very wonderful experience. And *no*, I am *not* going to tell you what it was. But it could buy you forgiveness for far worse crimes." He stooped and kissed her cheek. "Now — be off with you, before my reputation is wholly ruined. The thought of having compromised two young ladies at one and the same time, and one of them my own newly-betrothed cousin, is too much even for my sang-froid, while if James discovers your present whereabouts I shall undoubtedly receive a politely worded invitation to meet him in the cold, depressing dawn — and he a Marine and a first rate marksman! But don't forget to explain our arrangements to him in careful detail. Marines *do* so like to have their orders cut and dried!" With which parting jibe he pushed her hastily through the door.

Friday morning was warm and sunny. Damon suggested that they should have their island picnic that very day. Such weather was unlikely to last. Alethea was quite content, James and Marianne enthusiastic. "We'll use the skiffs," their host elaborated. "Means rowing out to the island, but with decent luck we'll get a breeze to sail home. Wind often gets up, late afternoon. Something to do with the hills, I'm told. Handle a skiff under sail?" This was directed provocatively at James who retorted that he was willing to back himself to be first home. Alethea couldn't imagine why the gentlemen found this amusing. Probably it had something to do with the differences between marines and sailors, which appeared to be a constant subject for laughing argument between them.

He was certainly the stronger oarsman. Having, by patient coaxing and much firmness, avoided Bellamy's attempts to join the party ("For she would certainly decide on swimming the last stretch — she always did — and your muslin would be soaked.") they were first to reach the island and had tied up at the tiny landing stage and carried the picnic hampers ashore before the second skiff came in James rested on his oars and called across to them. "Marianne wants to show me the water gardens. Don't eat all the lunch before we come back."

Alethea tensed nervously. She could scarcely suggest that she, too, would like to see the water gardens, since she had visited them twice already, though to be left alone with Damon was not at all to her taste, being precisely the situation she had taken care to avoid this week past. However he was unconcernedly busying himself with stowing the hampers in the shade of an overhanging bank and putting two slim-necked bottles to cool in the tiny stream that debouched into the lake at this point. That done to his satisfaction he turned to her in easy cheerfulness and enquired, "Now. What would you like to do, Man Friday? Laze in the sunshine, or explore the island?"

Exploration sounded safer, and was, in any case, more to Alethea's mind. It was a very miniature island, but it was easy to see what a paradise it had been for two small boys. They came at last to the log cabin which had been built close beside the spring that fed the tiny stream. Alethea looked at it with a feeling of sick dismay. In the whole of the vast Byram estate, this was the only corner that had been permitted to fall into disrepair. And in contrast with the beautiful maintenance elsewhere, the sad decay of this crude, childish play-house was heart-breaking.

There was a lump in Alethea's throat that had to be swallowed before she could say, hesitantly, "Couldn't we do something about putting it to rights? There are four of us."

Damon smiled at her, and flicked the crisp ruffle of muslin at her wrist with a careless finger. "In *that* dress? No, my dear, I think not." But his mind was working furiously. *This* he had not planned. Would it serve?

He said, quite pleasantly, "In any case it will not be used again. *I* shall not marry, *now*. And I believe you were privileged to hear Aunt Emily's prediction of what would become of Byram when my cousin Barnard inherited."

The latter part of this speech was lost on Alethea. Worn down by the strain of the past weeks, the thought that her painful sacrifice should be in vain was just too much. "But you *must* marry," she told him furiously. "Why else do you think I refused you?"

Through the long years ahead they were to laugh over and again at the memory of that speech. Damon was to hold it up as a perfect pattern of feminine logic. At the moment both were too vulnerable, too intent, to see its humour.

He said slowly, "I want only one woman in the world for my wife. If she will not have me, I will have none. And *she* refused me."

Still she was not sure. There had been that old affair that Tina had spoken of — some jade who had jilted him. But since then — She said breathlessly, "My lord — when you — when you did me the honour of — of — was there not some other lady whom you had in mind as your chosen bride? If the circumstances had not compelled you to offer for me?"

"Some other lady?" he said, as one wholly puzzled. "From the day of our first visit to Hampton Court my mind was increasingly set upon you. My mind — but not, I confess, my heart. I remember telling Marianne that at last I had chosen a bride. Arrogant, presumptuous oaf that I was! It was not until my chosen lady had utterly rejected me that she lifted me out of the depths with a kiss. A kiss that I will remember to my last breath. I learned in that moment how much I loved her."

There could be no more room for doubt. "Me?" said Alethea childishly.

His answer was to pull her into his arms. "You," he said against her mouth, and kissed her fiercely, a long hunger to assuage.

She responded as naturally as one who, after long wandering, has come home. It was Damon who at last put her from him and said on a shaken note, "How soon will you marry me?"

"Oh! Soon — very soon." And then, tentatively, "In the spring, do you think?"

"The spring! You call that 'very soon'! Come — in a months time?" he suggested coaxingly. And then, seeing her startled face, relented. "Forgive me, love. It shall be just when you choose. You will naturally want time to buy your bride-clothes. I had not thought."

Before she could explain that it was nothing of the kind, he went on slowly, "These two years past so many things have gone awry. First there was Edward. *You* will understand something of my feelings — our ships lying idle in New York while my brother was penned in Yorktown with Cornwallis's army. In the event we sailed the very day that the army surrendered, though Edward had, in fact, been killed several days earlier. Then there was the tragic business of my nephew. Once again I was too late to be of any use. Do you wonder that now, with happiness beckoning, I am greedy to lay fast hold of it before it vanishes from my grasp? I did not mean to spoil your pleasure in your preparations. I know girls set great store by such things."

Six months was quite a usual time between betrothal and marriage. Alethea had suggested the spring without thinking beyond the usual conventions. But here was a trouble that must be mended without delay. She slipped a hand into his. "I will marry you as soon as my parents will permit it," she said steadily.

He did not immediately answer, his brow furrowed in thought. She offered shyly, "I am not of age, you know, and may not marry without their consent."

The frown vanished. He turned and caught her up in his arms, kissing her so comprehensively that she was rosy and breathless when he put her down again, still keeping one possessive arm about her waist while his free hand tilted her face to his.

"A month it is, love," he told her eagerly. "It can just be done. We'll persuade your father to prolong his stay, so that he can marry us — *you'll* want that, of course. He can read our banns for the first time on Sunday. Then I shall have to leave you in his keeping because *I* must post off to bring your Mama — and Susan, of course. Your mother informs me that she is so much improved in health that she is sure she can safely undertake the journey if we do it in slow easy stages. *My* mother will be in the seventh heaven helping you with your frills and fripperies. She always yearned for a daughter. There! How will that fit?"

The girl in his arms had choked on a gasp of indignation. Now she said with dangerous sweetness, "So everyone but me knows all about it. Why! It's nothing but conspiracy! How well I read your character at our first meeting, Sir Arrogance."

He had the grace to flush, but he only gathered her closer. "It *was* a conspiracy," he admitted. "But your parents only promised their support if I could win your free consent. And I did, didn't I? Or don't you *want* to marry me?"

It was no good. She could never harden her heart against that engaging small boy appeal. And if one was going to yield, one might as well do it with a good grace. "I want it every bit as much as you do," she began, "but" — and the rest was lost in his kiss.

Presently they bestirred themselves to unpack the picnic lunch. "I do wish James and Marianne would hurry up," said Alethea, looking with interest at the appetising array. "I'm quite shockingly hungry."

"I'm afraid they're not coming, my love," returned Damon politely. "They asked me to present their apologies. A prior engagement, you know."

She cried out at that, but he only chuckled. "Didn't you hear James offering odds that he'd be first home?" he demanded. "I had to get you to myself for a while if we were ever to sort out our affairs, and this seemed the only way."

"*More* conspiracy," she said, but her tone was suggestive of amusement rather than scolding. "In fact, to all intents and purposes, you've abducted me."

"Well I had to make sure of you somehow," he pointed out, as one who has just accomplished a difficult task and expects praise for his virtue. "I'd already compromised you and *that* had no effect, so what else could I do? And you shouldn't really be surprised. Your father has been studying our family tree and he informs me that I'm descended from a long line of bad border barons. Men who were accustomed to take what they wanted and hold it fast."

And then, suddenly serious, "As I shall do, my darling. As I shall do."

*

THE END

Printed in Great Britain
by Amazon